Meddling in Manhattan

Book Two in At the Altar

By Kirsten Osbourne

Copyright 2015 Kirsten Osbourne

After the most recent in a stream of horrific blind dates, Addie's roommate suggests she see a professional matchmaker to try to find love, instead of allowing people who are less qualified to set her up. When she doesn't agree, her friend sets up a meeting without her knowledge. After meeting the woman, Addie decides to let her try to find someone for her, but she doesn't hold out much hope.

Jake watched his best friend find love through the services of Matchrimony, but doesn't consider it himself. He's persuaded to contact matchmaker, Dr. Lachele, by his friend and his wife. When he meets his new bride, he's thrilled with the match. Will they be able to get past his obsession with his work to find love? Or will they give up too quickly?

To sign up for Kirsten Osbourne's mailing list and receive notice of new titles as they are available, visit kirstenandmorganna.com

Chapter One

Addie Myers leaned forward across the table, talking animatedly about her work. She was doing the only thing she'd ever really wanted to do, and she wanted to share it with the world. She loved being excited about her work, unlike so many of the young women she knew. Just then, she was sharing it with the most recent man her roommate, Jennifer, had set her up with. "So every weekend, I teach a class in a different kind of craft to mothers and children. A kind of mommy and me class for crafts."

Bob continued acting as if he was paying attention, by staring straight at Addie's cleavage as he'd been doing the entire night. "Sounds cool." He'd said very little else in the hour and a half she'd spent with him so far. She was glad they had met at the restaurant, so she wouldn't have to let him escort her home. That would just drag out the time she was forced to spend with him.

She took another bite of her lasagna, trying to continue the conversation, but getting more than a little annoyed with the man. "What do you do for a living, Bob?" *Do you have a job, Bob? Do you work with the mob, Bob? Please don't make me sob, Bob.* When she was bored, she always made up rhymes in her head. It made her happy.

Bob tore his eyes away from her chest and finally met hers. She was certain it was the first time all night. If she asked him what color her eyes were, he'd probably respond with a guess as to her bra size. What a boob. "Huh? Did you ask me something?"

Addie closed her eyes and mentally counted to ten. "I asked what you do for a living?" It was a pretty typical first date question. She hoped he'd prepared an answer.

Bob shrugged, his eyes going right back to her breasts. "I'm a mid-level manager for a paper company. We do stationery and that kind of thing. Kind of boring really."

What a shock. Boring Bob has a boring job. She put her hand over her mouth to stifle the giggle over her rhyme. "Sounds fascinating," she lied. "How do you know Jennifer?"

"Oh, she's dating my brother. She didn't tell you?"

No, she didn't tell me. She also didn't tell me you were so obsessed with a woman's mammary glands, you were incapable of having a conversation. It's hard to believe that sweet Andrew has such a lecher for a brother. "I see." She finished her meal in silence, wondering if Bob would ever be able to tear his eyes away from her chest long enough to carry on a conversation.

After the waiter inquired whether they wanted dessert, she sighed. "I think maybe I should get a sticker with an eyeball on it to put on my chest, don't you?"

Bob shrugged again. "I guess so."

"That way we could make eye contact." She stood and picked up her purse. "I'll catch a cab. Good night, Bob. Thanks for the delicious meal and the titillating conversation."

Addie rushed out the door to the street, holding her hand up for a taxi. It was a cold March evening, and it had started to snow. She loved snow in November. By March? She was ready to never see another snowflake again. She climbed into the back of the taxi. "Where to?"

"Greenwich Street." She leaned back, trying to block out the smell of stale smoke. Closing her eyes she thought over her boring date. Why did her roommates insist on boring men for her? Did she really seem that boring? She knew she worked more than her share, but boring? She didn't think she was that boring.

When they'd arrived at her apartment she'd paid the cab driver. For a minute, she just stood there in the snow, her face raised to the heavens. Why was finding a good man so difficult? She had a degree in marketing, was a successful business-woman, not bad to look at...especially her breasts apparently. Why did she attract men like Boring Bob the Boob?

She'd never been anyone's idea of a sex object, though. She had dark blond hair and green eyes. She was slender, but not model slim. Like every other woman in the country, she wished she was thinner. No, she wasn't drop-dead gorgeous, but she didn't make small children run away in tears either.

She sighed and headed toward the main entrance of her apartment building. When she reached the apartment she shared with three other women who were also in their twenties, she unlocked the door, praying she'd be alone for a few minutes. That was a date she needed some time to recover from.

Her roommate Danielle was sitting on the couch with a tub of popcorn watching *Notting Hill*. She looked up at Addie. "Another bad date?"

Addie sank down onto the couch and took a handful of popcorn, even though she wasn't at all hungry. "It was awful. His name was Bob, and he spent all night starting at my chest. Boring Bob the Boob." She rolled her eyes. "What's wrong with me that I keep ending up with creeps like him? All I want is a regular guy who will treat me right and love me. Do they still exist?" She sure hoped they did, because she didn't want to spend the rest of her life alone.

Danielle paused *Notting Hill* on a close up of Hugh Grant's face. "You really want to know what I think?" Danielle was a petite blond who made Addie, at five foot four, feel like a giant. She was just tiny.

Addie took another piece of popcorn and chewed it slowly while studying her friend's face. "I don't know. Do I want to know what you think?" Danielle was working on her masters in psychology, and often her opinions hit too close to home.

"I think you're letting people set you up who have no business finding their own man, let alone one for a friend. You need a professional."

Addie let out a bark of laughter. "What? You mean like a dating website? There's no way!" She'd heard too many stories of creepy men who met women through dating sites.

"No, I mean like a professional matchmaker. A woman with a PhD in psychology who has a proven track record."

"Yeah, like someone like that exists." Addie rolled her eyes at the very idea of someone with that kind of education wasting her time matching people. It would be ludicrous!

Danielle grinned. "Well, I just happen to know

someone..." She turned sideways on the couch so she was fully facing her friend. "You know I'm doing my internship this semester with this bigwig relational psychologist?"

"Yeah..."

"She's got a matchmaking business on the side. It's called Matchrimony. Isn't that an awesome name?" Danielle was obviously excited at the idea. "What she does is she finds people, and after extensive interviews, she pairs them up. The catch is they meet *at the altar*. So like you for instance, you have a business here in the city, so she would either find you someone who works really close to here, or doesn't mind relocating. Then you'd see him for the first time while you're walking down the aisle. She's got a great success rate."

Addie shook her head adamantly. "There's no way! I let people set me up for dates and look at the freaks I end up going out with. Imagine what would happen if I let someone find me a husband, and I had no veto power. I couldn't do it!"

"Will you at least agree to meet her? I promise, you'll love Dr. Lachele. She's sweet and quirky and has purple hair. What more could you ask for in a matchmaker?"

"I don't think so. Thanks for the suggestion." Addie stood up and stretched. "I'm going to go take a bath, and wash the feel of Bob's eyes off my body. I'm going to take my iPad in there and watch a movie, so I may see you later, but I may not."

"Have a good bath!" Danielle called out as Addie disappeared into the bathroom. She stared at the door for a minute after it closed. Addie *needed* Dr. Lachele. More than anyone she'd ever met.

*****

Jake Roberts ignored the ringing of his phone. He was in the middle of a scene where a dragon was tamed by a beautiful princess. When the ringing stopped and started again immediately, he let out a growl and snatched his cell phone up, not bothering to check the caller ID. "What?"

"Sorry to disturb you. It's Scott."

"Is it important? I'm in the middle of a scene." Scott was his best friend, but he really wasn't in the mood to be disturbed by anyone just then.

"Want to call me back when you're done?"

Jake sighed. "No, I'll get back to it. What's up?" He wandered into the kitchen of his small house and snagged a Coke from the fridge, glancing out the window. It was dark. How had that happened?

"Savannah wanted me to invite you over for dinner tomorrow night. She said that you're just to the point in your book that you are probably forgetting to eat again."

Jake started to protest, but he was sure Scott could hear his stomach growling, so there was no point. "Sure. I can do that. What time?" He did need to eat, and he loved his best friend's new wife. Besides, he hadn't seen their baby in a couple of weeks. He needed to take the little rug rat a couple more books.

"About six?"

"I'll be there." Jake hung up without another word. He needed to get some food in him and finish his scene. He felt drawn back to the computer as if it was a magnet, but stopped and shook his head. "No. I need to eat first!"

Wandering back into the kitchen, he checked the refrigerator. There were more Cokes but little else. Opening the freezer, he hit the jackpot. A frozen pizza. While it cooked, he could finish up his scene. Perfect.

*****

Jake got to the ranch just before six the following evening. He banged on the front door, a gift for the baby under one arm, and a dozen daisies in his other hand. Savannah opened the door with the baby cradled in one arm. She took the flowers and inhaled deeply. "Thank you, Jake." She stood on tiptoe and kissed his cheek before wandering into the kitchen to put the flowers in water.

Jake knew her well enough to know to follow her to the kitchen. "How old is Kaeden now?"

"Three weeks." She expertly put the flowers in water using only her free hand. Carrying them to the table, she put them in the center. "There. Perfect." Glancing down at the baby, she smiled. "He's asleep. I'm going to put him down." She wandered to one of the small bedrooms on the first floor of the huge ranch house and put Kaeden in a bassinet before closing the door softly, careful not to wake him.

"I made a bison stew," she told Jake as she wandered back into the dining room.

"Oh, yum. I need something hot!" He looked out the window. It was snowing again. He was sick of the snow. "Where's Scott?"

"He's taking a shower. He'll be down in a minute."

They chatted about his book and the baby for a few minutes until Scott joined them, his hair still damp from the shower. "Hey, Jake."

Jake nodded to Scott. "I've decided to run away with your wife. You want us to take the baby or leave him with you?"

"Oh, leave him with me," Scott said. "I know she can live without me, but she won't last without the baby."

Savannah laughed, as she served the stew into bowls which she carried to the table. "I made a loaf of fresh bread to go with it."

Jake was practically drooling. "I need a woman to take care of me. I don't care what she looks like just so long as she remembers that I need to be fed every few hours."

Savannah and Scott exchanged a look. "I think you should talk to Lachele at Matchrimony," Scott told him. The two men had been best friends since childhood, and he knew if anyone could convince him to do something as stupid as calling a matchmaker, it was Scott.

Jake laughed. "Sure."

Savannah leaned forward. "We're serious. Jake, you don't trust anyone, because you're afraid all women are after your money. If you meet at the altar, that worry is gone. Why not at least talk to her?"

Jake looked back and forth between the two. "Well, I know it worked for you two, but really? How could she possibly find a woman for me?" A woman who would put up with being ignored ninety percent of the time for a computer. Women just didn't go for that kind of thing.

"Just ask her!" Savannah insisted.

Jake sighed. "Fine. I'll call her as soon as I finish my book." He had at least two weeks to go on it. They'd probably forget by then.

Savannah shook her head. "After dinner."

"It'll be too late in New York to call after dinner."

She gave him the woman look that Jake knew meant she knew he was just making excuses. "I'm not going to let you forget on purpose, Jake."

"Forget on purpose? What does that even mean?"

"Jake? You're calling her after dinner." Savannah handed him the plate with the bread on it, and he took a piece, recognizing the futility of arguing.

*****

Addie wove her way through the restaurant. Danielle had texted her that she was waiting at a booth in the corner. She spotted her friend's blond hair, but who was with her? Wait...hadn't she said the woman she worked for had purple hair? She frowned, but decided to give her friend the benefit of the doubt. Maybe Dr. whatever-her-name-was had forgotten her lunch and hadn't wanted to eat alone.

She slipped into the booth beside Danielle. "Hey! Did you order for me? I only have an hour."

"I got you their baked potato soup. No chives." Danielle grinned at her. "You always get the same thing."

"Doesn't everyone?" Addie looked at the woman across from her, noting her sparkling green eyes and her purple hair. "I'm Addie Myers."

"Hi, Addie. I've heard so much about you. I'm Dr. Lachele Simpson. Most people call me Dr. Lachele."

"It's nice to meet you, Dr. Lachele. I've heard a lot about you too. Do you enjoy your work?" It felt strange eating lunch with two people who had made psychology their life's work. She wasn't up for being psychoanalyzed during her lunch hour.

"Oh, yes. I love introducing two people who I

know are meant for each other. It satisfies me in a way nothing else ever could." Dr. Lachele's voice was soft and sweet. Addie felt drawn to her immediately, in a wary sort of way. If she hadn't been so nervous around her, she thought the woman would make a great friend. "Why don't you tell me about yourself, and we'll get the ball rolling."

"What ball?" Addie looked at Danielle. "I told you I wasn't willing to be set up!"

"Good Gravy, Danielle! You could have at least told me that so I wasn't coming here blind." Dr. Lachele gave Danielle an annoyed look. "You know better than to force someone to talk to me!"

Danielle had the grace to look ashamed. "Normally I'd agree with you. You don't know Addie, though. She keeps getting set up with these losers. Who was the guy last week, Addie? Boring Bob the Boob, wasn't it?"

Addie shook her head. "Jennifer set me up with him!" Why was she being blamed for Jennifer's mistake?

"Give Dr. Lachele a chance. She's really good at this." Danielle leaned over and whispered. "I think she already has someone in mind for you."

Addie sighed. "I guess we can at least talk, since you've already wasted your time by coming here."

She was intrigued at the idea that Dr. Lachele may have someone picked out for her. She wanted to find the right man.

Lachele looked back and forth between the two friends. "I won't force you to do anything you don't want to do, Addie."

Addie crossed her arms over her chest. "That's good, because I won't do anything I don't want to do. I don't know what kind of women you usually work with, but I assure you, I'm self-confident and know how to think for myself."

Lachele nodded. "Do you mind if I take notes while we talk?"

*****

Once the process was started, Addie was amazed by how quickly everything went. In mid-April, she went to her parents' house to talk about what she'd done. The youngest of seven children, Addie was nervous to admit to her parents that she was going to be walking down the aisle in less than two weeks toward a man she'd never met. At this point all she knew was that he lived in Montana, and he was flying there to marry her. It wasn't a lot to go on.

Her mother brought cookies and coffee from the kitchen like she did every time someone visited. Her mother had been forty-two when she was born, so she was now approaching seventy, and she had the silver hair to prove it.

Addie took the cookie and leaned back in her chair, trying to find the right way to explain what was happening. She'd rehearsed the conversation fifteen times on the subway on the way over, but still, she felt at a loss for words.

"I'm getting married," she finally said after her parents had filled her in on her brothers and sisters and nieces and nephews.

Her mother squealed, clapping her hands together. "Oh, I'm so happy for you! I didn't even know you were seeing anyone. When do we get to meet him?"

Addie took a deep breath. "You can meet him the day of the wedding. It's a week from Saturday." She wanted to close her eyes to escape from the looks on their faces, but she couldn't do that. She had to act like she wasn't at all nervous about what she was doing.

Addie's father looked at her with a worried look. "You didn't get yourself in trouble, did you?"

She smiled at her father's old-fashioned phrase.

"I'm not pregnant, Dad."

"Why can't we meet him before the wedding?" her mother asked, looking confused.

"He lives in Montana," Addie replied, saying a quick prayer that they wouldn't ask any more questions, but she knew they would. They always did.

"How did you meet a man from Montana?" her father asked. "Was he here on business? Vacation?" They knew she hadn't left the state in a good long while.

Addie sighed. "I haven't actually met him yet. We're meeting at the altar."

Her father got to his feet. He was a retired New York City police officer, and was still in tip top shape for his age. "What do you mean you haven't met him?"

Addie looked down at her hands. She hated disappointing her parents. "One of my roommates works for a woman who runs a matchmaking business where people meet at the altar. She tricked me into meeting the woman, but it didn't take me long to agree to let her find just the right man for me." She shrugged, wishing she could convince them. "I've gone out with so many men over the years, and not one of them was interested in marriage. I want to get married and start a family. You two have always been such a shining example of how a marriage should be. I'm ready to stop looking and start living." There, maybe flattery would work.

"What's the name of this business?" he asked, still standing over her as if he was going to decide to discipline her at any moment.

"Matchrimony."

"I'm going to research it. See what I can find out. If I find that it's a bad company, do you promise not to go through with it?"

"Of course!" Her father had been a police officer for many years. She trusted him implicitly.

"All right then. Do you know the man's name?"

She shook her head. "No. I'll find that out on my wedding day."

A slow smile spread across her mother's lips. "I'm so glad you're going to give it a try. I've been worried you'd be alone forever. Just make sure your father checks him out before the wedding."

"I promise. It'll be all right."

*****

Addie sat at the back of the church, wearing her eldest sister's wedding dress. Her parents had convinced her that she shouldn't buy a dress when she wasn't sure the marriage would last. She didn't tell them that she'd signed a contract agreeing to spend at least a year with the man if she went through with the ceremony. She had until she said, "I do," to change her mind, but after that, she was legally bound to stay with him unless he hurt her somehow.

"You're going to be fine. Dr. Lachele is really good at what she does. You're going to be so happy," Danielle told her, squeezing her hand tightly.

"I hope so." Addie looked at Danielle, wearing a dress in a soft pink, a bridesmaid dress she'd worn for another wedding. "I'm nervous." Saying the words aloud just made everything worse. She wanted to kick herself for not pretending everything was just fine.

"You'd be stupid if you weren't. You're about to marry a man you've never met. But trust me. He's going to be right for you."

Dr. Lachele breezed into the room then, surveying the situation. "Good gravy, girl! You're not getting nervous now, are you? Why, I found the man who's just right for you. I'd go so far as to say that he was put on this earth just for you."

"But I don't even know his name!" Addie exclaimed. For her, that was the hardest part. She didn't care what he did for a living or what he looked like, but she hated not knowing his name.

Lachele sat down in a chair opposite Addie, stroking a stray hair from her face. "His name is Jake. And he's going to take one look at you and think he's got an angel walking toward him."

Addie frowned. "And then he'll realize that I'm head strong and belligerent at times, and he'll decide it's a fallen angel he found."

Lachele laughed, shaking her head. "Not Jake. He's not going to be terribly easy to live with, but it's going to be worth it. Trust me. He's your soul mate."

Addie wasn't even certain she believed that soul mates existed, but she just nodded to humor the older woman. "I'll take your word for it."

"I gave his name to your father, because he wanted to have him investigated before the wedding. So we're going to be delayed by about thirty minutes while he runs a background check." Lachele shrugged as if the delay meant nothing.

"What if he's planning on whisking me off to Tahiti as soon as we marry?" Addie asked. She'd planned for a week off after the wedding. Her assistant manager was perfectly capable of running the shop, even though Addie had rarely taken a day off.

"Then you'll have to catch a later flight," Lachele told her. "Besides, I told him to plan on spending the night here in New York tonight. The first Matchrimony wedding ended with the couple running for a flight to Montana. I don't think a bride should have to worry about leaving her own reception early just so she can catch a flight. Do you?"

Addie shook her head. "I guess not." She wasn't certain she'd ever be ready to leave the reception. What if the man repulsed her? She wouldn't want to actually be alone with him. What if one of his eyes was made of glass and he kept giving her a funny look? What if he had fifteen other wives spread throughout the country?

Lachele got to her feet. "You're going to love Jake, which is a good thing."

Addie frowned as she watched the other woman run toward the door. "Why is that a good thing?" As long as they were able to stay together, the woman had done her job, right?

"Because I need more Matchrimony munchkins, of course."

Addie looked at Danielle after the door had closed. "She's full of energy...but she's odd."

Danielle shrugged. "She's more than a little crazy, but that doesn't mean she's not good at matchmaking."

"I never said it did!" Addie protested.

It was right at half an hour later when Addie's father came into the room. "He's an interesting man, but no criminal record. You should marry him."

When her father said nothing else, Addie wondered what he was hiding. "And?" She wanted to know every detail her father had found out. Why wasn't he disclosing everything?

"You agreed to marry a stranger. I'm not giving you details." He looked at Danielle. "Lachele said you need to get your sweet cheeks out there, so you can walk to the front of the church first."

Danielle jumped to her feet and hurried from the room.

Addie looked at her father. "You're really okay with this?"

Mr. Myers nodded. "I couldn't be more okay with it. He's a good man."

Addie got to her feet and smiled. "Thank you for checking him out for me. It makes me feel like I'm going to be safe." Not that she wouldn't be anyway. In her eyes, her father was equivalent to Superman. If she called him and told him something was wrong, he'd be there in moments.

He kissed the top of her head. "You're a beautiful bride. Don't tell your sisters, but you outshine every one of them."

Addie smiled, certain her father had said the same thing to all three of her older sisters on their wedding days. "Thank you, Daddy."

He offered her his arm as they left the room, walking toward the door at the back of the sanctuary. Addie forced herself to breathe slowly, extremely nervous now that the time was here. She was about to walk down the aisle to a stranger she'd be spending the rest of her life with. What was she thinking?

At Lachele's nod, the back doors of the sanctuary were flung open, and the entire congregation got to its feet. She walked slowly down the aisle, her hand clutching her father's arm harder than it should have been. She couldn't get past her nervousness.

Her eyes went to the man at the front of the church, who was staring at her with a half smile on his face. He was a tall man with dark hair and brown eyes. They seemed to twinkle at her as she walked.

She couldn't believe her luck. Why on earth would such a nice-looking man be searching for a bride through a matchmaking service like

Matchrimony? Why, he was handsome enough, she was sure women fell at his feet.

Once they reached the front of the church, her father placed her hand into Jake's and the two of them took the three steps up to stand before the pastor.

"Dearly beloved. We are here under unusual circumstances as we join this man and woman in the holy state of matrimony. Not many couples are able to agree to meet each other for the first time mere minutes before they exchange vows, but that's exactly what this couple just did. They set eyes upon one another as she stepped into this sanctuary and started her long walk down the aisle toward the man she'd spend the rest of her life with...a man she'd never before laid eyes on."

Addie looked at Jake to see how he was reacting to the pastor's words and saw that he was looking right at her. He hadn't taken his eyes off her since she'd stepped into the sanctuary, and she never wanted to stop staring at him. Surely it was a good sign that they found one another so physically attractive, wasn't it?

She repeated her vows as instructed, and accepted the ring he put onto her finger. It fit perfectly. Lachele must have provided him with her ring size.

When he kissed her, it was as if the world

stopped for just a moment. The kiss was short, but for all its brevity, it caused more rioting emotions than she'd ever experienced. Yes, she was meant to marry this man.

Chapter Two

Addie took Jake back to the bride's room as soon as the ceremony was over. She wanted at least a few minutes to talk to her new husband. She didn't even know what he did for a living! Not that it mattered. She didn't believe in divorce, and she'd signed a contract not to separate for a year.

When they got to the room at the back of the church, Jake did what he'd wanted to do in front of the entire congregation. He pulled her into his arms for a real kiss.

He put his hands at her waist and looked deeply into her eyes. "I didn't want to embarrass you with a real kiss in front of everyone."

Addie felt breathless as she stared back at him. His eyes were a deep chocolate brown, and she felt as if she could be lost in them. "You didn't?"

He shook his head. "No, but we're alone now."

Her mouth turned up into a slow smile. "We do seem to be alone. I wanted to talk for a minute, but I guess that can wait." She was babbling, and she wished he'd kiss her to shut her up. She'd never been so nervous, or so excited, at the idea of a kiss before.

He stroked her cheek with his index finger. "You guess?" He slowly lowered his head.

Addie had enough of waiting, she wrapped one arm around the back of his neck and pulled him down for a kiss. As soon as his lips touched hers, she felt electricity shooting through her body. She moved closer to him, her breasts pressing against his chest. Never had she felt so much passion. Even when she'd kissed other men, she hadn't felt this strongly. How had Dr. Lachele known he was the one for her? What magic formula did it take to see two people, apart, and know they were meant to be together?

Jake let out a low groan and lifted his head. "Who'd have thought Lachele knew so much about matchmaking?"

Addie grinned, leaning her head against his shoulder. "She was certainly right with us." She took his hand and led him over to two chairs, sitting beside him. "Can we talk for a minute?"

He shrugged. "Do I have to stop touching you while we talk?"

She laughed softly. "I'd rather you didn't!" She couldn't believe how strong the attraction was between them. She turned to face him. "Dr. Lachele said you live in Montana?"

He smiled. "I currently live in King, Montana, which is a small town outside of Billings. I've lived there my whole life, but I'm open to moving." He was not only open to moving, he coveted the Manhattan Library. He'd move into it if he thought he could get away with it.

Her eyes widened. "You are? I was hoping you'd say that!" She frowned. "What about your job?"

"Oh, that's not a problem. I'm a writer." He watched her face carefully as he said it, hoping he wouldn't see dollar signs appear in her eyes. For some reason, people thought that if he was a writer, he made a boat load of money, which wasn't necessarily true. It was in his case, but it didn't have to be.

"Oh," she said with a frown. "I can't make ends meet on my own. Will you be able to help with the bills at least a little?" She'd known a few people who called themselves writers, but they'd had to wait tables to make ends meet.

Jake blinked a couple of times at her misunderstanding. He started to correct her but immediately thought better of it. Better if she thought of him as an impoverished writer trying to put out his first or second book. "I can help some. Couple thousand a month?"

She sighed with relief. "Oh, that's great. That'll be enough with what I make. I found a little apartment, but it's just out of my price range on my own. With that added to my income, we'll be fine." She didn't mind helping him reach his dream by taking on the bulk of the bills. He may eventually have to get another job, but for now, they'd be fine.

Jake couldn't believe how excited he was at the prospect of getting to know her without his money being a huge issue. He was almost as excited about that as he was to get back to the hotel with his new bride. "Good." He lowered his head and kissed her again. "How soon can we get away from here?"

Addie blushed. "We have to go to the reception. My whole family is out there." But she wanted to be alone with him too. She was a twenty-five year old virgin, and she was convinced she was lacking in some way. She'd never even been tempted to sleep with one of the men she'd dated. Of course, two or three dates was all it had ever been for her.

Jake sighed. "Fine. We'll go to the reception, and I'll pretend not to be fantasizing about removing that beautiful dress from your body." Normally Jake wouldn't have been so forward, but she was his wife. He could say what he wanted.

She was sure even her shoulders were blushing at

that point. The dress she'd borrowed from her sister left her shoulders completely bare, so she was sure he knew how embarrassed she was. "I think we should be around other people. We'll talk more later."

He grinned, happy that he could make her so uncomfortable. He considered it a good sign. "Much later. I have a feeling other things are going to need to take precedence for me." He got to his feet and took her hand in his. "Let's go greet everyone."

As they walked toward the church's fellowship hall, she was very aware of the man at her side. She had signed a contract to spend the next year of her life with him, no matter what. It was good so far, but was that only because their hormones were running rampant?

Her mother made a beeline for her as soon as she stepped into the room with the rest of the guests. "Are you all right? He didn't hurt you, did he?"

"Mom, we just talked. He's a nice man." Addie turned to Jake. "Jake, this is my mother, Carolyn Myers. Mom, this is Jake." Her mother had seemed all for the wedding the last time they talked. Hadn't her father told her that he'd only discovered good things during his investigation?

Her mother nodded. "It's nice to meet you. My husband was a police officer and still has a lot of connections. Just so you know." With that, she turned and walked away.

Addie was mortified. "I'm sorry. She's really freaked out about me marrying a stranger."

"Want to know a secret?" he asked, his lips close to her ear.

"What?"

"I didn't tell my parents."

"Would your mama be freaked out too?" Addie asked, giggling softly. She could just picture a tiny little woman with white hair chasing after him with a frying pan, telling him he shouldn't marry a stranger.

"Definitely. She'd be calling you Lizzie Borden by now, convinced you'd murder me in my sleep." He didn't add that his mother would think she'd murder him for the money. Did that really matter?

She introduced him to her brothers and sisters and finally her father, who shook his hand. "I want you to know I had you investigated," her father said.

Jake nodded, his eyes meeting the older man's. "I assume you found nothing negative?" Did he know about his pen name? Jake knew it was a matter of public record.

Mr. Myers shook his head. "Nothing. I'll still be keeping an eye on you, but for now, you have my blessing."

"I'm happy to hear that, sir. I'll take good care of your daughter." He hadn't realized he'd be so nervous meeting her father. Of course, he was the man who would be taking the other man's daughter to bed that night. It was an odd relationship.

"I trust that you will." Billy Myers smiled at his daughter. "You know where to find me if you have any trouble."

Addie smiled. She didn't know why her father being overprotective made her feel safe, while her mother doing the same thing just made her angry. "Thank you. I'll be fine." She squeezed Jake's hand which had been in hers since they walked into the fellowship hall.

"Where are you taking her for a honeymoon?" Billy asked, his eyes on Jake.

"We're going to a small resort in South Dakota known for its healing waters. In fact, the name means healing waters."

Addie looked at Jake. "I didn't realize we were going anywhere. That sounds interesting."

Jake shrugged. "It's off the beaten path, and the same family has owned the place since 1874. I went to college with the man who runs it now. Kyle McDonough. He was a good friend."

Addie nodded. His friend must have gotten him a discount. She was glad he knew how to be frugal. "I only have a week off work."

"That's fine. I was only planning to stay for a week. I'd go crazy if I had to take longer than that off work myself."

Billy eyed Jake. "What city is the resort in? I want to know where you're taking her."

"It's called Whisper Creek. It's not really a city, just a small town. Closest decent sized city is Rapid City. It's got a lot of character. I've been a few times." Jake studied Addie. "Did you pack for a honeymoon?" He could think of things he hoped she'd packed, but he'd be just as happy seeing her in nothing at all.

She nodded. "Yes, and I packed for any weather. I have bathing suits and ski suits." She shrugged. "I'll condense what I really need into one suitcase, and we can drop it at the new apartment on our way to the airport."

"That works for me." Jake looked at her father. "Do you want my cell phone number? Would that make you feel safer?"

Billy nodded. "Yes, I think it would. Then I have two numbers to reach the two of you at."

"Oh, I have an idea," Addie interjected. "I

brought both suitcases here to the church. If I condense into one suitcase, would you take the other home with you, Dad? It would make it easier for us tomorrow."

Jake nodded. "It would. Our flight is at nine. It would make it a lot easier."

"I'd be happy to."

"Okay, I'm going to go move the winter clothes into one suitcase and summer stuff into another. I just need summer stuff, right? Do I need any dress clothes?" She was mentally going through everything she'd packed. Why hadn't she thought to put all the cold weather clothes into one suitcase and the warm weather into another as she was packing? She should have thought ahead. Usually she was a great deal more organized than this.

"There are nice restaurants we'll go to. I'd pack lots of shorts and a couple of nice outfits." Jake cared almost nothing for clothes, but he could tell his little bride would want to be dressed correctly for everything.

"If you'll excuse me, I'll go pack." She squeezed Jake's hand and smiled at her father.

Jake looked at her. "I'll come with you."

Thinking about the nightgown she'd packed for their wedding night, she shook her head quickly.

"No, it's fine. I'll be right back." She hurried toward the door, hoping he'd take a hint and not follow her.

Jake watched her go with a frown. What could she possibly be hiding from him? Her father had already walked away, so he wandered over to where Savannah and Scott were standing in the corner. Dr. Lachele was holding Kaeden, fussing over him.

"She's getting the stuff she needs all into one suitcase for the honeymoon," he said to no one in particular. He just didn't know anyone else, and he didn't want to look stupid standing alone in the middle of the room at his own reception.

"What do you think of her?" Savannah asked, keeping her voice soft.

"She's gorgeous! She seems smart. I have no complaints." Jake watched the door, hoping she'd come back through it.

"Oh, you will," Scott told him. "Even Savannah and I had a rough patch at first. It's hard being married to a total stranger, even if you know you're supposed to be a good match." Scott winked at Savannah.

Jake grinned, remembering how clueless Scott had been at first. "Well, I'll do my best to make her happy. I'm sure we'll be fine." He knew better than to accuse his wife of having PMS if she got angry with him for doing something stupid.

Dr. Lachele looked up from the baby. "You will. Just remember, no separating for the first year, because you two will have it all figured out by then. And I need more Matchrimony grandbabies, so hurry up on that."

Jake shook his head. "We've only been married for a couple of hours. Slow down!" He had no desire to add babies to his brand new marriage. He wanted time to savor his wife first.

"No. You hurry up! I need dozens, please."

Jake looked at Scott. "I'm not having dozens of babies. Are you having dozens of babies?" He wasn't going to bend to the will of a crazy purple-haired woman. He didn't care if he had known her his entire life.

Scott shrugged. "Probably not. But if she keeps matching couples up, she'll get her dozens."

Savannah laughed. "I'm not having dozens, but a few more would be really nice."

Scott swallowed hard. "How many is a few? I didn't much like watching you go through labor!"

Savannah linked her arm through Scott's and leaned into him. "Another four or five maybe?"

Scott shook his head adamantly. "Two more. That's my final offer."

Savannah rolled her eyes but said nothing.

Lachele looked back and forth between the couple who had almost reached their one year anniversary. "You tell him, Savannah!"

Addie rejoined them then, going to stand beside Jake, who automatically wrapped an arm around her shoulders. "All done. Dad has my suitcase, so we're all set." The only strangers at her wedding were right in front of her. They must be Jake's friends.

Jake looked at her with a grin. "Does that mean we're ready to go?"

Addie blushed, knowing exactly where his mind was going. "You could introduce me to your friends first!" He was certainly in a hurry to start their honeymoon. It was embarrassing that he was so openly enthusiastic about it.

Jake sighed. She was going to insist on staying a little longer. "This is my best friend since childhood, Scott Ward. Scott, this is Addie."

Scott held out his hand. "It's nice to meet you, Addie. You've got a good guy."

Addie smiled. "I think so. Of course, I'll let you know how I feel about him in a couple of months."

She was very aware that she would be annoyed by some of his traits. She had never known a married couple who didn't get annoyed over toothpaste. All the fights seemed a bit different, but they were all about toothpaste.

Scott grinned. "I know how you feel. Savannah and I were married in this same church a year ago. Lachele fixed us up too."

Addie's eyes widened. "You're a Matchrimony couple? How's it going?" Her first instinct was to grab Savannah by the arm and drag her off, asking how things had gone, but she couldn't do that.

Scott looked down at his beautiful blond wife. "It's wonderful. I'm happy. She's happy unless I'm doing something stupid, which happens more than I care to admit. We're good right now."

"You already have a baby! And you've only been married a year?" Addie didn't want things to happen so quickly for her. Slow and steady when it came to babies.

Savannah grinned. "We both wanted children and saw no reason to wait."

Addie looked up at Jake. "I want to wait at least a year before we start trying!"

Jake nodded, more relieved than he could express. "That sounds good to me. It's not something we need to decide at our reception."

Addie smiled, but inwardly she disagreed. It needed to be discussed before the wedding night. She'd gone to the doctor for birth control, and she didn't want to deceive him by making him think there was a chance they'd have a child when there wasn't.

Dr. Lachele looked at Addie. "You have my number for when you need me, right?"

Addie frowned. "When I need you? You mean if?"

Savannah laughed. "She means when. Trust me on this. Jake's a good guy, but it's just a matter of time. A New York woman and a Montana man are bound to clash."

Addie eyed Savannah. "Maybe I need to get your number as well."

"Oh, you definitely do. In fact, I already wrote it down for you." Savannah handed a small card in an envelope to Addie. "Feel free to call me during reasonable hours."

"I will." Addie clutched the envelope, knowing she'd need the moral support of the other woman. The situation was too strange to go through alone. She would need someone who understood.

Jake looked at Scott in mock-fear. "Should we

allow this? They won't plot against us, will they?"

"I'll let the 'allow' comment slide, because you don't know me well," Addie said mildly, winking at Savannah who grinned.

Jake raised an eyebrow. "You don't think it's your job to obey my every whim?" He didn't think that a man should be 'in charge' of a woman either, but he wanted to see her reaction.

"No, I really don't." Addie looked at Lachele, playing along with the teasing. "Why don't you screen these men better, Dr. Lachele? I'm going to have to get a divorce before I even have a honeymoon."

Lachele looked up from the baby. "You'll do fine." She nodded to Scott and Savannah. "If those two could make it, anyone could."

Addie looked at Savannah again, wondering what had happened between the other two.

Jake interrupted her thoughts. "We're going. We've dallied long enough."

Addie raised an eyebrow at her new husband. "Dallied? You use dallied in regular conversation?" It wasn't that she didn't know and like the word. She just didn't know anyone who actually used it.

"I'm a writer. I use lots of words in regular

conversation." He shook hands with Scott. "Thanks for flying out to be my best man."

Scott nodded, a smile on his face. "Anytime. You just let me know when you need me, and I'll be there."

Addie hugged Savannah. "So nice to meet you. I'll be calling you!"

"I'll be waiting for the call!"

Jake and Addie made the rounds, saying their goodbyes. Carolyn glared at Jake over Addie's shoulder. "Be careful. Call me if there are any problems. Your father will be on the next flight."

"I'll be fine, Mom!" Addie turned to her father and hugged him as well. "Don't worry about me."

Billy hugged her back. "I'm not worried. He's a good man. You'll do fine."

Addie was surprised her father had become a supporter of Jake, regardless of what he'd found in the man's past. He was usually a great deal more skeptical.

They went to get her things from the bride's room. "I checked into a room at a hotel before I came here. I hope that's all right."

Addie was surprised when he named the hotel. It

was a legendary New York City hotel that was certainly out of her price range. "That's wonderful. How could you afford that?" She knew the question was rude, but she wanted to make sure he wasn't spending money he shouldn't on the expensive hotel.

"I have connections." Jake wasn't certain how long he'd be able to keep up the 'starving artist' charade, because he tended to like the creature comforts.

He hailed a cab, showing her he'd spent some time in New York previous to that day. When had he been there? "You've been in New York before?" she asked.

"I was here for Scott's wedding and ended up extending my stay because of the Manhattan Library."

Addie smiled. "One of my favorite places in the whole world!"

His eyes lit up as he faced her in the backseat of the cab. "Really? You're a reader?"

She nodded. "I'm a voracious reader. I thought about having a small second-hand book shop after college, but instead decided on my craft store."

"Tell me about your store." He loved to listen to her talk about anything.

Addie smiled. "Well, my craft store is different than any other I've ever seen. It's not tiny, but it's not big either. I sell craft patterns, both new and second hand, and I offer support. I only sell crafts that I, or someone on my staff, knows how to do well, and we're there to lend a hand. We have classes that teach each of the crafts. For instance, I have a crochet class I teach every Tuesday afternoon, and I teach a mommy and me paper crafting class on Monday mornings." She frowned. "I'm not home a lot, because my job is very demanding." If he couldn't understand her need to work, they'd never last.

"I understand having a demanding job. The voices in my head don't let me stop until I've put enough words on paper to satisfy them."

"The voices in your head? You realize that makes you sound more than a little bit crazy, right?" She liked it though. Well she liked it as long as her parents didn't hear it and come unglued.

He shrugged. "However it makes me sound, it's true. I have all these stories that want out, and I have to make it happen. I'll go nuts otherwise."

"Then you should make the stories happen." She leaned her head against the back of the seat, facing him. "Do you enjoy writing?"

"So much. I think I'd do it even if no one ever bought a single book. I just need to be able to get them out of my head." He reached out a hand and used his index finger to trace her upper lip. "I'm not a poet, but you make me want to write odes to your beauty."

"Odes to my beauty?" She giggled a little. "It's going to take me a while to get used to the way you speak."

Jake leaned over and kissed her softly. "I'm more worried about how quickly you'll get used to my touch."

She blushed. "I don't think that's going to take nearly as long."

The taxi driver pulled up in front of the hotel, and Jake got out, holding the door for her. He paid the driver, and then walked around to the back of the taxi to take her suitcase. "Thank you," he called, holding her hand firmly in his as he pulled the suitcase into the hotel.

He headed straight for the elevator, hoping she wouldn't need to eat, but realizing she probably would. They'd only served cake at the reception. "Are you hungry?" he asked.

Addie put her hand on her stomach. She was hungry, but she was also nervous. She wasn't sure if she could eat. "A little."

"We could get room service."

"I'd like that."

They got off the elevator and walked down the hall to a room on the right. He inserted his key card in the door and held it open while she stepped inside.

"Oh, wow!" She looked around the room in amazement. She'd heard a great deal about the hotel, but she'd never imagined she'd stay in a room so lovely. "The view is awesome!" She slid open the door to the balcony and stepped out. She loved Manhattan late in the afternoon. It felt so special to her. She couldn't imagine living anywhere else.

Jake set her suitcase on a bench in the room and followed her out to the balcony. He wrapped his arms around her waist and rested his cheek atop her head. "I can't believe we're really married."

She smiled, leaning back against him. "I can't either. It all happened so fast."

"What made you decide to go see Dr. Lachele?" he asked, wondering how a beautiful woman like her had ended up meeting a man and marrying him at the same time.

"It all started with a man I like to call Boring Bob the Boob...You see, my roommates were constantly setting me up with different men. Most of them were pretty worthless. I lived in an apartment with three other women. One of them, Danielle, worked for Dr.

Lachele. I went out with this absolute creep who wouldn't stop staring at my chest, and he couldn't manage to string a sentence together because he was so busy ogling me. That's how he got his name."

"Boring Bob the Boob?" Jake grinned, the writer in him loving the alliteration. The husband in him wasn't pleased to hear that the man had been staring at his wife's breasts, but they hadn't met at the time, so he couldn't complain too much.

"Yes. Boring Bob the Boob. Anyway, when I got home from that awful date, my roommate Danielle told me about Dr. Lachele. She suggested that the reason I kept going out with losers was because I kept letting people who had no idea what they were doing set us up. I told her I wasn't desperate enough to see a professional matchmaker and marry whomever she found for me on sight."

"You did? How did we end up here then?"

"Well, the following week, Danielle asked me to meet her for lunch, and Dr. Lachele was there, thinking I was ready to hire her. It took us a minute to connect, and at first I was furious with Danielle, but I listened to Dr. Lachele, and decided I could agree to at least give her a chance." She sighed, actually happier at this moment than she thought she'd be. She felt so comfortable with Jake. It was as if she'd known him a great deal longer than she had.

"I'm glad you did." His words were simple, but they carried a lot of weight.

She turned to him, a smile on her face. "I'm glad I did too."

He leaned down and kissed her, his tongue tracing the outline of her lips. His hands went to her narrow waist, pulling her flush to his body. She was still wearing her wedding dress, and all he could think about doing was peeling it off her. He backed into the hotel suite, having left the door standing open behind him. He turned once they were inside, not breaking the kiss, so he could close the sliding glass door that led to the balcony. He moved them toward the couch, which he knew was beside the balcony door, sitting on it and pulling her into his lap. "I want to make love to you," he whispered against her lips.

Addie was surprised at the heady feeling of power at his words. She'd never before felt like she had so much power over a man. She sank into his kiss, her lips parting for his tongue. Her hands tugged at his jacket, pulling it off his shoulders, before removing his tie and unbuttoning the top button of his shirt for him. He couldn't be comfortable in the restricting clothes.

Jake was thrilled at her actions, and his hands went to the tiny buttons running up and down her back. He wanted to groan, hating the idea of having to slowly maneuver each button out of the hole. As he was struggling with the second button, his finger rubbed against a zipper. Were the buttons just for show? Why would someone do that?

Sure enough when he tugged at the zipper, her dress opened at the back, and his hand slipped inside, only to encounter a slip underneath her dress. He wanted to touch bare skin!

"Stand up," he whispered, breaking the kiss. "I want to get this off you!"

Addie blushed, but she stood, turning her back to him so he could push the dress off and unfasten her strapless bra, before turning her back around to face him. When she stood before him in just her panties and stockings, which were held in place by garters, her face was red. She forced her hands to remain at her sides, trying not to cover herself in her embarrassment.

Jake's eyes traveled her body from head to toe. She had full breasts, a narrow waist, and wide hips. Everything about her was just perfect in his eyes. "You're beautiful," he whispered reverently. "I've never seen such a beautiful woman in my life."

"I..." Addie swallowed hard. She needed to tell him, but she wasn't sure how. Would he mind? "I've never done this before."

Jake's eyes widened, and a slow grin transformed

his face. "You're a virgin? I didn't think they even existed anymore."

She nodded. "Does that bother you?" She'd never felt comfortable enough with a man to let him touch her so intimately. She'd only known Jake for hours, though, and it felt right to her, even as it felt wrong. She was so confused!

He shook his head. "Of course not." He got to his feet, cupping her face in his hands and kissing her softly. Scooping her up into his arms, he carried her into the bedroom, setting her on her feet next to the bed. "I want to teach you all there is to know about lovemaking." He finished unbuttoning his shirt and removed it, tossing it on the floor. He kicked off his shoes, ignoring where they landed. His socks came next, because he didn't want his new wife to see him without his pants on for the first time when he was still wearing socks. How stupid would that look?

He unbuttoned his pants and dropped them to the floor, watching her eyes as they went to the tent formed at the front of his boxers. He could see she was nervous, but he had no idea how to soothe her. "You okay?" he whispered softly.

She nodded. "Just a little scared," she answered honestly.

"Don't be. We're both going to enjoy this!"

Chapter Three

Jake pushed Addie back onto the bed, following her down. He'd get rid of his boxers later, when she was less nervous about what he was about to do to her. His lips toyed with hers for a moment while one hand went down to cup her breast, his thumb stroking her nipple. "You feel so good!"

She let out a soft moan. She'd never let another man touch her bare breasts as her new husband was doing. She now knew it had been smart to have that rule, otherwise she could have let things go too far. She was shocked at how sensitive her nipple felt under his thumb. She wrapped her arms around him, her hands roaming over his back. She was surprised at the muscles she found there. He must work out, because no man could get this strong by writing all day.

He broke off the kiss and rolled to one side, propped on his elbow. He let his free hand continue to toy with her nipple, his eyes on her face. "Do you like that?"

She nodded, biting her lip to keep from crying out. It felt strange letting him touch her that way, but oh so good. Something that felt this good had to be wrong!

"Is there anything you want me to do?" he asked, his eyes on hers. He wanted to take things slowly, because he didn't want to hurt her, but his body was screaming at him to hurry.

She had no idea how to answer that question. She'd never done this before, but she assumed he had. "I don't know!"

He chuckled softly. "Okay, how 'bout this? I'll do what I want to do, and if you don't like it, you tell me to stop."

"Is that even possible?" she asked, before covering her mouth with her hand. Had she really just said that to him? She knew it was the twenty-first century, but she'd been raised to have strong morals. It was odd that anyone would touch her this way, and it would be all right. Even her husband!

He raised an eyebrow. "That bodes well for our lives together." He got to his knees and slid her garters down her legs, and then slowly rolled her stockings down and off her feet. Once the stockings were on the floor, he brought her foot to his lips, kissing the arch. "You are the most beautiful woman I've ever seen."

She shook her head, unable to force her tongue to respond. His lips were causing sensations she'd never dreamed she'd feel to shoot up her legs and into her core. She spent well over forty hours a week on her feet, leaving her feet tired and sore almost all the time. His kiss made them suddenly feel alive with energy.

After a moment, he dropped her foot and moved to her hips. "Raise up." When she did as he told her, he caught the band of her panties and pulled them down her body, dropping them on the floor.

Once she was fully nude he simply stared for a moment, unable to believe his luck. He'd agreed to marry a woman sight unseen, and she was prettier and more special than any he'd ever met. God was certainly watching over him.

He moved back so that he was beside her, his hand going back to her breast, while his lips toyed with hers. "I'm the most blessed man alive," he whispered against her lips.

Addie closed her eyes, enjoying how cherished he made her feel. And how hot. She couldn't discount how hot he made her feel. His fingers felt like magic against her skin. She nipped at his neck, her teeth scraping his skin, and he let out a groan.

He kissed a trail from the corner of her mouth, down her neck, and to her breast. He took a moment to touch the tip of her breast with his tongue before taking the nipple inside and suckling.

She arched off the bed toward him, her hands clutching his hair to keep him close. She felt restless and wiggled on the bed, not sure what she was supposed to do, but knowing the feeling was too intense for her to remain still.

His hand trailed down her stomach and to her thigh, one moving between her legs to stroke her. His thumb went to her nub, rubbing it gently, while he carefully inserted a finger, his lips never leaving her nipple.

All of the sensations at once made Addie crazy. She lifted her hips to meet his hand, moaning softly.

Jake was encouraged by her reaction, moving his thumb faster. He wanted her to reach her pleasure before he caused her the inevitable pain. He kept his eyes open as he suckled, watching her face. He could tell she was close to her climax, so he moved his thumb a little faster, and she clenched around his hand.

He removed his boxers and knelt between her legs, reaching a hand down to guide himself to her entrance. He pushed in quickly, thrusting through her maiden head, trying to make the pain quick.

Addie moaned softly as he hurt her, but the pain

was gone before she knew it. It wasn't exactly pleasurable for her, but because she'd felt so much pleasure before, she didn't complain.

Soon he'd rolled off her and was gathering her in his arms, raining kisses over her face. "You're an incredible woman, Mrs. Roberts."

Addie smiled, snuggling close to him. She may not have enjoyed it as much as he had, but she enjoyed being close. Right then? That was all that mattered.

She laid in the curve of his arm for a long time after, listening to the sound of his heartbeat. She couldn't believe she'd just done that with a total stranger, and that she'd enjoyed it so much.

"Tell me what you write," she finally said, once the silence had grown uncomfortable.

He turned to face her on the pillow, his hand stroking up and down her bare arm where it stuck out over the top of the sheet. "I write science fiction."

"And you like it?" She couldn't imagine the work that went into writing a book, especially a book where she had to create her own world as was the case with most science fiction. She was an avid science fiction reader, so she was familiar with the genre.

He nodded. "I do. I have a series of books about

dragons that I write." He deliberately didn't mention the name of the series, because if she read science fiction at all, she would recognize it.

"How many hours a day do you write?" she asked. The idea of someone writing books, taking nothing and creating something, fascinated her. It was so similar to what she did with her crafts, yet still so different.

"Anywhere from fourteen to sixteen," he answered honestly. "I'll try to keep it to fourteen when you're around."

She blinked. "How do you find time to eat?"

He shrugged. "I don't always. Scott used to come over once a week just to make sure I got fed. Now I don't always remember until I'm done working for the day."

"Don't your hands hurt at the end of it?"

"A lot of times, they do. I have a lot of problems with tendonitis, but I take ibuprofen for the inflammation. Sometimes my eyes quit working by the end of the day. My back is always killing me from being bent over a keyboard. The voices in my head don't care. They want the words out. And my fans? They finish a book and an hour later ask when the next one will be out. Sometimes I just want to scream at them that I just finished a book, and they should give me a week to glory in the finished product, but I know that's never going to happen. They think I should write until my eyes bleed." He gave a half laugh. "I'm being overly dramatic. They don't really believe that, but sometimes, I think if it meant they got their books faster, they'd feel that way. Human limitations are tough."

"You have fans? Really?" He must be more successful than she'd initially thought.

He nodded. "It's strange. I mean, I'm just this boring guy from King, Montana, and I have fans all over the world."

She made a face. "None of them ever stalk you or try to find you, do they?"

He shook his head. "So far I've avoided the science fiction conferences and stuff, so no one knows what I look like. I write under an assumed name, so no one knows who I really am. I like living a quiet life."

It sounded to her like he must be quite successful to have the kind of fans he'd mentioned, but she didn't say anything. Maybe writers had to be terribly successful before they made any kind of real money. "Well, I promise not to tell anyone that you're a writer. It'll be our little secret."

He grinned. "You can tell Scott and Savannah.

They already know." He leaned forward and kissed her nose. "And I owe you an apology. You told me you were hungry, and I said we'd order room service, and instead I dragged you off to bed right away."

"I wasn't exactly kicking and screaming!"

"No, you weren't, and that makes me very happy." He rolled to his side and out of bed, striding naked across the room to get the room service menu which he brought back to the bed. "What are you hungry for?"

She'd been only slightly hungry earlier, but now she was downright peckish, to use a British word she loved. "Why don't you get me all of page three?"

He laughed. "All of page three, huh? Without even looking to see what's on page three?"

She sat up beside him on the bed, making sure she kept the sheet tucked firmly under her arms to conceal her breasts. She rested her head against his shoulder as she read the menu as well.

"You know it doesn't matter if you keep them covered, right?" he asked, a gleam in his eye.

"What?" she asked, pretending she didn't know what he was talking about.

"You don't have to keep your breasts covered. I've licked them and touched them enough that I know their exact shape and look. There's no need to bother."

She blushed, shaking her head at him. "Well, that wasn't exactly gentlemanly of you to point out, was it?"

He laughed, the sound filling the room. "Maybe not, but guess what?"

"What?"

"I liked looking at them, touching them, and licking them. I'm not going to pretend I didn't."

Addie decided to ignore him, as she read over the menu. "Can I get a burger, fries, cheesecake, and a Pepsi?"

"Pepsi? Are you kidding me?"

"No, I love Pepsi."

He groaned. It was one of the rare hotels that carried both Coke and Pepsi products. "I'm a Coke lover. I don't know how we're going to make this work!"

"So if I accidentally spill Pepsi all over myself, you won't lick it off?"

He grinned at her. "If anything could make me a Pepsi lover..." He picked up the phone for room service. "How do you want your burger?"

"Medium well." She got up to use the restroom, and pulled the sheet off the bed, wrapping it around her completely sarong style. She wasn't going to walk around naked. She'd leave that for him.

*****

An hour later, they'd eaten and set the dishes out in the hallway for the housekeeping staff to pick up. She wasn't certain what she was supposed to do. It wasn't quite bedtime yet, but she hadn't brought her computer to do book work on. Since opening her store, she had spent all her time at home doing the store's financial work. Adding the daily numbers, calculating costs, working on payroll. It took a couple of hours every night. Added to the number of hours she spent at the store, there was little time for anything else.

"Tell me about this place we're going to!" she finally said, wanting to hear about her honeymoon location.

"Oh, it used to be one of those fancy places where the idle rich would go to 'take treatments' back in the 1800s. Now, it's been restored to be as much like it was back then, but with the modern touches we need. There are carriage rides throughout the grounds, and the hot springs are available to soak in. We can rent horses and go horseback riding, or even wander to an old fashioned looking mercantile that has the 1880 price of everything right alongside the 2015 price. That's one of my favorite places to go. I love to learn about history!"

"Oh, it sounds wonderful!"

"It is. The decor is something straight out of a history book, but hidden behind little panels are plugs for our chargers. The bathroom has a beautiful old fashioned claw foot tub with hot and cold running water. The lobby is the same as it was the day they opened, and you sign in on this giant register. Of course, they keep the computers out of sight, but you can tell they're tapping away at the keys when they're checking people in."

She smiled. "I'm going to love it!"

"I really think you are. I love the restaurant, because the servers dress in the same uniform they used back in 1874 when the resort opened, but people can dress however they want. All of the furniture is antique, and they use real glass dishes. They do their best to keep up the illusion of being in the 1870s. I love it there."

"We fly out tomorrow?"

"Yeah, we fly out in the morning, and we will

come back a week from tomorrow. Then you go back to work Monday?" he asked, wondering if he would go nuts not writing for that long. He could dictate into his phone if he just had to, and he could also write with pen and paper if he got really desperate. He didn't want her to think that his job would always come first.

"Yeah. My assistant manager will cover everything until then, but I'm going to be on call. I don't think she'll bother us unless it's life or death, though." She studied him for a moment as she cuddled into his side on the couch. "I work sixty hour weeks, and then come home and work some more. Is that going to bother you?"

He wanted to jump for joy. She was just as much of a workaholic as he was. Lachele *did* know what she was doing. "That's fine. I really work at least that much, so I'm not going to get jealous of your work." He just hoped she wouldn't get jealous of his.

She wondered absently if he'd cook since he'd be home alone all day, but she didn't ask. It just made sense that he'd put dinner on. "Good. It was the one thing I was worried about."

"Honestly, I was worried about the same thing with the kind of hours I keep. I don't need a wife who gets angry every time I sit down to work."

"Do you ever have problems with writer's

block?" she asked.

"I don't even believe it exists. Writing is five percent making up stories and ninety-five percent putting your butt in the chair and doing the work. I've met so many people over the years who call themselves writers because they come up with stories and write a chapter or two. That's not writing. Writing is putting in the hours to tell the entire story beginning to end." He sighed. "And I'm on my soap box again. Tell me to shut up, would you?"

She laughed. "I have better ways to shut you up." She knelt on the couch beside him and cupped his face in her hands as he'd done to her. She kissed him softly, her tongue stroking into his mouth.

After a moment she pulled away, resting her forehead against his. "Effective?" she asked.

"Oh, very effective. Why, I'd let you use those methods all day..."

*****

They left for the airport early the next morning, and Addie was extremely excited to see the healing waters. He hadn't told her the real name of the place, because he said he couldn't pronounce it. It was a

French name. She was sure she'd see it on a sign somewhere.

They'd gone to the shore a lot growing up, but she'd never been as far west as South Dakota. She wondered if they'd have a chance to see Mount Rushmore or any of the touristy places in South Dakota while they were there.

At the airport, they waited their turn, and she was surprised to find out he'd booked first class seats for them. She was beginning to wonder about his finances. Was it possible that he had an inheritance from somewhere? How was he able to afford all the extravagances? She hoped he hadn't over extended himself with their honeymoon to impress her.

He let her have the window seat on the plane, and she was excited. She'd never flown, and it was fun watching the clouds go by. They had a connecting flight in Salt Lake City. By the time they landed in Rapid City it was late afternoon. Addie was surprised at the size of the airport in Rapid City. Even the airport in Salt Lake City had seemed tiny in comparison to JFK. He rented a car as if he flew all the time. She frowned watching him. He certainly didn't act like a struggling writer.

On the drive to the resort, she watched out the window, marveling at how flat everything was. "It's like another world. I have a hard time believing we're in the same country."

He laughed softly. "I feel the same way about Manhattan. Where I live in Montana, there's nothing. Billings is the big city, and it's tiny in comparison. I love Manhattan, though. Nowhere else in the world has a library like that. Not that I've seen anyway."

"You only married me for my library," she joked.

"Oh, no. That's not true. I married you for your breasts. I'm just not as obvious about it as Boring Bob the Boob."

She laughed. "Bob was a real treat. And you're allowed to stare. We're married."

"And touch? I'm allowed to touch too, right?"

"Don't push it!" She was grinning as she watched out the window again.

When they reached the resort, she tried to read the sign. It said Les Eaux de Guerison-Place of the Healing Waters. She didn't speak French either though, and decided to abbreviate it to Healing Waters. She wasn't going to twist her tongue in knots trying to say a name that obviously was never meant to be said.

When they walked in the front doors, a man rushed over to them and pounded Jake on the back. "Well if it isn't the famous science fiction writer. When's the next book coming out?"

Jake groaned. "When it's done, freak. How's the little missus?"

"Pregnant." The man, who must have been Jake's college friend said with a grin. "Very very pregnant."

"You can't be very pregnant. Pregnant is one of those things you are, or you're not. Kind of like dead. You can't be very dead. You're either dead, or you're alive."

"Writer," the owner snarled.

"Businessman," Jake returned with a scornful curling of his lip.

Addie decided to ignore what the men were saying to each other, so she wandered off, looking around the hotel. It was huge, and just as Jake had said, was decorated in the manner she would have expected from an 1874 bath house. The walls and railings of the two story building were white, and there was a large red woven area rug on the floor with gold accents.

Jake joined her a few minutes later as she stood gazing at a painting of a woman in an old fashioned bathing costume. "Do you want to wear one of those?" he asked.

She laughed. "If I could look as beautiful as that woman in it, I would do it in a heartbeat."

"You'd look a million times more beautiful." His words were sincere. "Let's go to our room and get unpacked. Do you want to go in the waters, or swim in the pool? We could go for a horseback ride? Or we could nap. Napping is always an option." He waggled his eyebrows at her in a way that told her there would be no sleeping done if she chose the nap option.

Addie yawned dramatically. "I'm really tired. I think a nap may be in order." They'd reached their room by that point, and he unlocked the door with the key he'd been given. Unlike most hotels, the resort still used regular keys.

Once she'd preceded him into the room where their luggage was already placed, he pulled her close. "Nap sounds good to me too. Do you want to nap on top of me? Or do you want me to nap on top of you?"

She giggled as he kissed her, knowing exactly how this nap would turn out.

Chapter Four

By Saturday evening Jake and Addie had done a bit of everything the resort had to offer. She had shopped in the old mercantile, ridden horses, gone for a romantic carriage ride one evening, and spent more hours than she could count partaking of the healing waters. She felt closer and closer to her new husband every day, so happy they were getting along so well.

For their last night, Jake had requested a picnic hamper from the kitchen and they had taken two of the horses on a ride across the rolling hills. Finally, they'd found a place for a picnic, and they'd spread the quilt the resort had provided onto the ground.

Addie dug into the hamper finding plates, glasses, a carafe of lemonade, fried chicken, potato salad, and pickles. There was even a pound cake for dessert. She piled food onto both plates, and handed him a fork to eat with. "They really outdid themselves with this. I didn't see on any of the brochures that we could request a picnic," she told him.

"Oh, it's not a regular service they provide. They just do it for me, because I'm friends with the owner."

Which was part of the truth. The other part was that he bribed them a more than respectable sum to do it for him. "Are you ready to get back to the real world?"

She shrugged. "I'm ready to see how my assistant did while we were gone. I'm surprised she didn't text even once." It had been everything Addie could do not to text and check in on her, but she knew that Bailey was a capable woman, and she didn't want her to think she was watching over her shoulder. "What about you?"

He shrugged. "I've had a wonderful time here. I'm glad we were able to get away to get to know one another, but I'm starting to get itchy to get back to work." He'd taken a paper and pen into the bathroom the day before, and written a couple of pages the old fashioned way. He didn't want her to know how much he *needed* to be working while they were on their honeymoon.

"Will you work as soon as we get home tomorrow? Or will you wait until Monday morning?"

He hadn't even considered waiting. "Would it offend you if I got to work tomorrow evening?" He hoped it wouldn't, because he didn't want to start their marriage off by sneaking out of bed to go to his other love—work!

"Oh, not at all! All of my stuff was moved to the

apartment while we were gone. I'm going to have unpacking to do, and I know I'll want to call my assistant manager. No, home means business as usual." She shrugged. Just because she was married, didn't mean she could neglect her duties.

Jake breathed a sigh of relief. Good. She had the same kind of work ethic he did. They would get along just fine.

*****

When Addie unlocked the apartment the next day, she looked around in amazement. She'd asked her former roommates, sisters, and brothers to help with the move. Obviously they'd done so much more than she'd expected. She'd thought to walk into an apartment with boxes everywhere, but it was neatly arranged, even her knick knacks were out.

On the counter was a note, saying that Danielle had done it as part of her wedding gift. She suggested they use the time they would have spent unpacking wisely. Addie grinned, knowing she would do just that.

Jake had shipped a bunch of things from Montana, sending them to Lachele. The two women must have gotten together, because his things were put away neatly as well. He spotted his laptop at a desk in the corner of the room, and as soon as he saw it, he was mesmerized. He sat down, turned it on, and he forgot about everything around him.

Addie laughed as she watched Jake become reunited with his computer. She went into the bedroom and called Bailey, catching up on the happenings from the store while she was gone. Once that was finished, she went to her own laptop and did the paperwork from the week using the information Bailey had emailed to her daily.

When she was finished, she called Jake's name, but he didn't even notice, so she walked into the kitchen to fix something for supper. She frowned. There was nothing to fix. She walked back to her computer and ordered groceries to be delivered. There was no point in living in a huge city if you didn't take advantage of the delivery options there.

She went into the bedroom to call her mother while she waited for the groceries to be delivered. "Yes, everything's fine. We just got back from South Dakota. The resort was amazing. It was like stepping back into the 1870s. Truly a once in a lifetime experience."

"He didn't hurt you, did he? He treated you all right?"

Addie blushed, knowing her mother was talking

about the wedding night and wanting to have no part of that discussion. "He was great. I have no complaints. Really, I think Dr. Lachele found the right man for me."

She could hear her mother sigh. "Well, I hope it continues that way. Most marriages don't last, and you're starting out with a huge handicap not knowing the man you married."

"I'm getting to know him quickly. Don't worry."

"Well, your father checked him out, and he says he's a good man."

Her dad got on the phone then. "You have a good time, Addie?"

Addie smiled, happy to hear her father's voice. "Yes, it was wonderful. South Dakota is beautiful. We stayed near the Black Hills, and I had no idea they were so pretty."

"I checked out the area when he gave me the name of the resort. I'm sure it was nice. Did they really make it feel like you were in the nineteenth century, like they said?"

She laughed. "All except the indoor plumbing. That made it pretty obvious what century we were in. I felt like I had the best of both worlds."

"Good. Do you go back to work tomorrow?" he

asked.

"Yes, I do. I've already talked to Bailey. She said everything went well while we were gone. I've caught up on paperwork. Just waiting for groceries to be delivered now."

"That's my girl, always throwing herself at work and getting things done. I'm glad you're home."

"I am too. I had a lovely time, but you know what they say. The best part of getting away is always coming home!"

"You'll have to come for dinner one night this week, so we can see for ourselves he didn't murder you in your sleep." Her dad's voice was full of laughter, but underneath it, she knew he was concerned.

"Well, it's going to be a busy week at the store. How 'bout on Sunday when we're closed?"

"I'll tell your mother to expect you then. After church?"

Addie hesitated. She and Jake hadn't really talked about going to church. She knew he was a Christian, but he gave her the impression that he typically worked seven days a week until his eyes bled. "I'll let you know about time later in the week. Will that work?"

"Yeah, that's great. We'll see you Sunday."

Addie hung up the phone and wandered back to the kitchen, familiarizing herself with where everything had been put. She'd chosen a tiny apartment, barely six hundred square feet, so Jake was writing in the living room. She walked up behind him and peered over his shoulder, curious about the story he was writing.

Jake was in the middle of a huge scene when he felt her behind him. "What are you doing?" he asked, trying to keep the irritation out of his voice.

"I'm just curious about what you do," she said with a shrug.

"I write words. Lots of them. But I can't do it with someone watching over me like that. It's creepy." He knew his words would sound harsh to her, but he hated to be interrupted, and the sooner she learned that the better. His work was the most important thing in his life.

Addie bit her lip, wondering why he was upset with her. "I'm sorry. I'll find something else to do."

She wandered into the bedroom, trying her best not to get upset. She hadn't expected the harsh reaction to just seeing what he was writing. She couldn't believe it was such a big deal to him.

She found a book from the shelf beside the bed,

and laid down on her stomach to read it. It was a science fiction book by her favorite writer, Roger Holiday. She hadn't gotten to his three latest, but they were lined up on her shelf just waiting for her. Within minutes, she'd forgotten all about her new husband's surly attitude and was deep into her book.

The doorbell ringing startled her, but she hurried to the door, opening it wide for the groceries to come in. She looked over and saw that Jake was still tapping madly away at his keys. He sounded like a machine gun, and she wanted to ask how fast he typed. He was truly a speed demon.

Once the groceries were paid for, and the tip had exchanged hands, she put the groceries away, trying to decide what to make for dinner. She quickly decided on one of her favorite chicken dishes, and started the preparations. She sang softly as she worked, enjoying the idea of eating her first meal at home with her new husband.

She sat at their tiny bar, the only table in the apartment, reading her book while she waited for the food to cook. When it was finally ready, she served it on two plates, put a candle in the middle of the bar, and set everything just so. She wanted everything perfect. It was their first meal in their new home after all.

When she was finished, she called his name. "Dinner's ready!"

She waited a minute, and when there was no response, she walked over to Jake, saying it a bit louder. "Dinner's ready."

When he didn't respond again, she put her hand on his shoulder. He looked at her with a confused expression. "Yeah?"

"Dinner's ready!"

Jake nodded. He always ate while he worked. "Oh, good. Thanks. Would you bring it to me?" There was a clear spot to the left of his keyboard. That would be perfect.

Addie stood wavering for a moment and finally walked to the counter, blew out the candle she'd lit, and brought him his plate, fork, and a glass of Coke. "Anything else I can get you?" she asked in her best waitress voice.

"No, that's good. Thanks." He didn't even look at her as he continued pounding away at the keyboard. She wasn't even certain he knew she was there.

She sighed, walking back to the counter and sitting down to eat. Their honeymoon had been great, but she wasn't certain if she could handle him ignoring her all the time.

She ate in silence, rinsing her dishes and putting them in the dishwasher. She put up the leftovers, thinking he could eat them for lunch the following day, before looking over to see if he was ready for her to wash his plate and utensils. His food looked untouched, though, so she went to the bathroom to take a bath with her book. It was going to be a long night.

She'd made it through more than a third of her book before she stood up to go to bed. She'd been reading on the couch, thinking that if she was in the same room with him, he'd realize she still existed.

Finally she stood, walked to where he was, and again put her hand on his shoulder. Obviously she was going to have to touch him to get his attention. "I'm going to bed," she said in a soft voice. She'd put on a new nightgown she was certain he'd like and waited for him to look at her in it. At least he knew she was there when they were making love.

"Good night. I need to finish this chapter before bed." He didn't look up.

Addie stared at him in disbelief. "Good night." She went into the bedroom, feeling more rejected than she ever had in her life. She shut the door, not wanting to hear the keyboard, and climbed into bed. Closing her eyes, she wished for sleep. Who would have thought it would take only a week of marriage to become invisible?

*****

Addie woke alone the following morning, surprised to see the spot on the bed beside her untouched. Had Jake slept on the couch? She couldn't imagine why he'd be mad at her.

She got up and wandered into the living room, and there he sat, typing just as frantically as he had the night before. She didn't ask any questions as she fixed breakfast, making him a plate of eggs, toast, and bacon. She wondered if he'd gotten up, but she could tell he'd gotten himself more water, and his plate from last night was lying in the sink. There was an empty bag of chips beside him.

She walked over and put the plate beside him and went to get him a glass of orange juice. When she set it beside him on the desk, she put her hand on his shoulder. "I made breakfast."

His eyes flickered to her. "What time is it?"

"Eight. The store opens at ten, so I try to be there by nine-thirty."

"Oh. I guess I wrote all night." He took a sip of the orange juice. "Thanks for breakfast." He turned back to his computer and started typing again.

"Would you mind starting dinner this evening?"

she asked. "I have it all made up, you just need to put it in the oven at seven. It's a foil wrapped glass baking dish on the bottom shelf in the fridge. Cook it at three-fifty for an hour."

"Yeah, sure." He kept typing.

Addie shrugged and ate her own breakfast, getting ready for work. Her employees had a uniform, but she tended to dress in slacks, comfortable shoes, and a nice blouse. She glanced at him as she was leaving. "Don't forget to start dinner at seven, all right?"

"Yeah, sure."

While she was gone, he worked. He took a break around noon and napped for two hours before getting back to it. He'd promised the book would be completed by the end of the month, and taking a week off for his honeymoon had put him way behind.

*****

On the subway ride home, Addie couldn't help but wonder if she'd done something wrong. Jake had been perfectly attentive during their honeymoon, and she'd even thought he was starting to care for her, but as soon as he'd arrived home, he'd started typing like his life depended on it.

Everything had gone even better than she'd expected at the store while she was gone, so she took the plunge, deciding to give up the six day work week she'd had for years, and drop down to only working Monday through Friday. Her assistant could easily handle the store on Saturdays.

She couldn't wait to tell Jake that they'd have two days together every week instead of just one. Yes, she knew that a lot of the housekeeping chores would need to be done on Saturdays, but at least they'd be able to work on them together.

She opened the door, expecting to smell the dinner she'd worked hard to put together the previous evening. Instead, she saw Jake sitting at his computer, typing madly, and she could smell nothing. "Did you start dinner?"

He ignored her, typing away. She took a deep breath and counted to ten, walking to him and putting her hand on his arm. It took him a minute, but finally he looked up. "Oh, you're home."

"Yes. Did you put dinner in the oven like I asked?"

"Dinner? You didn't ask me to put dinner in the oven. What are you talking about?"

She frowned. How could this be the same man

she'd spent last week with? "This morning, after I gave you your breakfast, I asked you to put dinner in the oven at seven."

"I didn't hear you."

"You said, 'Yeah, sure.' You had to have heard me!" Why was he lying? If he forgot, he should just tell her he forgot to do it.

"I never heard you. Did you ask while I was typing?" he asked, frowning, trying to understand what had happened.

"Yes, but we had just been talking, and you *responded!*"

He sighed. "If I'm typing and you need me to do something, you need to have me repeat it back to you, so you know I really heard you."

"Are you kidding me? So you're responding to me without even listening to my questions? Why would you do that?"

He shrugged, realizing he was in over his head. He got to his feet and reached out to hug her. "I'm sorry. I've learned to ignore everything that happens around me when I work. I call it 'being in the zone.' It keeps me from being totally derailed by distractions."

She stiffened in his arms. "So not only did you

stay up working all night instead of coming to bed with me, you spent all day working and didn't even start dinner. You realize that we're married, and it has to be a partnership, right?"

His first thought was that she should be staying home, cooking all the meals, and doing the cleaning anyway, but he bit his tongue. He couldn't say that to her. He'd married her knowing she was a career woman, and he needed to support that. "I do realize that. I'm just on deadline..."

"And your deadline makes it all right for you to ignore me and pretend that you heard me? Are you kidding me?" She put her hands on his chest and pushed him away. We've been home for twenty-four hours, and you've done nothing but sit at that computer. That's not how marriage works! I put dinner together, you could have at least shoved it in the oven so we'd have a hot meal!"

Jake rubbed the back of his neck. "I've lived alone for ten years. I forget sometimes that there's life outside of the stories in my head."

"Well there is! I—" She took a deep breath, realizing she was going a little off the deep end. "I hope that you'll be more understanding of what I need you to do in the future."

"I will. I promise." Jake hoped he could live up to his promise. It was hard to remember there were others around, though. Why, he'd forgotten about his best friend's wedding, and Scott had packed his clothes for him, while he finished a scene. They'd barely been on time for their flight.

Addie needed to calm down before she said something she really didn't mean. They were never going to be able to work things out if she was constantly angry with him. "Would you put dinner in the oven at three hundred fifty degrees while I shower?" she asked, keeping her voice calm. Showering always worked to calm her.

At his nod, she went into the bedroom and chose an old pair of pajamas to change into. She needed to be comfortable, because he seemed to be over sex anyway.

When she was finished with her shower, she stood in the bathroom for a few minutes, still fighting her anger. She blow-dried her hair, dressed, and finally went out into the living room.

The smell of dinner filled the air. That was better. Jake wasn't at the computer for a change, instead he'd set plates on the counter and poured drinks for them. "Is there anything else I should make to go with it?" he asked, referring to her casserole in the oven.

"I was just going to make a salad with it." She walked toward the refrigerator, but he stopped her.

"No, you sit down, and I'll fix it."

She was surprised but not stupid enough to argue with him. She sat on one of the stools and watched him work.

He moved with the fluid grace of a natural athlete, something she'd noticed before. He didn't seem the type to belong to a gym. How did he stay in shape? "Do you work out?" she asked.

He shook his head. "Well, for one week out of every month, I do, but I don't think that counts. I tend to go for walks to clear my head when I'm first starting a book, because I need the extra input." He shrugged. "Mostly I just work."

"Why would you work out for one week every month?" she asked. That didn't make sense to her at all.

"Well, I have a very strange writing schedule. I tend to work three weeks out of the month, and then take one week off. So I work sixteen or eighteen hour days for three weeks straight. Sometimes I work twenty hours per day. Then my brain just kind of melts, and all creativity is gone. I work on marketing, and admin stuff during that week, but I also go to the gym, I take long walks and make it to the grocery store. When my three weeks start up again, I don't starve to death. That kind of thing." He mixed the salad while he talked, his movements efficient. He obviously knew his way around a kitchen.

He served both of their salads and took the stool beside her, turning to her before he ate. "I want you to know that I really am sorry about not starting dinner. I do that sometimes, and I'll try not to, but I'm not sure that I can stop. When I get involved with my work, I just can't seem to hear or comprehend what's going on around me. Let's hope there's never a fire while I'm working, because I just don't think I'd notice."

Addie nodded. "I understand all that. What infuriated me is that you responded to me as if you were listening when you weren't. I just felt ignored and lied to all at once. Of course, I was still hurt that you didn't even notice when I put on something sexy for you before bed last night and you never once glanced at me. That's not supposed to happen a week into marriage."

He frowned. "I missed that? That's not good!" He tilted his head to one side to study her. "Want to put it on again later and see if I notice?"

She pretended to think about it for a minute. "Not particularly." She took a bite of her salad, smiling inwardly. He needed to see how it felt, didn't he?

He grinned, realizing what she was up to. "Doesn't matter. What you're wearing looks pretty darn sexy to me. I'll just take that off you."

She laughed. "This is an old, faded pair of pajamas. I know it's not sexy."

"Yeah, but there's a hole...and it's in a very interesting place."

She refused to look for the hole, but she knew her face turned bright red. "Behave yourself."

He shook his head. "Women! You behave yourself around them, and they get their feelings hurt. You start acting frisky, and they get all offended. How are men supposed to know what to do?"

"Do you want a hint on how to understand women better?" she asked, leaning toward him as if she was about to impart a huge secret.

"Yeah, how?"

"Read our minds!" She got up and walked over to rinse her salad bowl and put it in the dishwasher before taking his and doing the same.

Jake watched her with a grin on his face. Being married to Addie was never going to be boring.

Chapter Five

Jake didn't work anymore that evening, giving Addie his complete attention. He did the dishes, and they sat together on the couch talking. "When do I get to see your store?" he asked. He was being polite, and he was certain she knew it. He really did want to see the store eventually, but he didn't have time right away. Hopefully she wouldn't mind if he waited a few weeks.

She shrugged. "It can wait until you're ready for your break, I guess." She wanted him to see it, but now that she understood his routine better, she could wait the three weeks until he was ready to take a long break. "My parents are expecting us for dinner after church on Sunday." She hoped it didn't make him angry that she'd agreed without checking with him.

He wanted to groan, but he didn't. "Okay. Do you want to go to church as well? Or just go over there after they're out?" He would go to church if she wanted him to, but he was more of a solitary worshiper. He needed the time to work on his manuscript, but he owed it to her to do what she wanted on that. He should have explained his work routine while they were on their honeymoon, instead of waiting for her to see it.

"I'd like to go if you don't mind. I've always attended church regularly, and it would feel weird if I didn't." She turned more fully toward him so she could see his face during their discussion.

He nodded. "That works. And then how long will we be at your parents' after church?" How long would he be away from his work? He was going to lose at least half a day from what he could tell. If he could keep up the pace he had going, the whole book would be done by Sunday evening. Maybe he could get some extra words in before that.

She frowned. "Do you want to board up the door and live here like a hermit?" Was he really that work driven, or was he anti-social as well?

That was exactly what he wanted, but he was certain she didn't want to hear it. "Not all the time. I mean, there's time for going out and being around friends. Most of the time I want to be home with just you, though." Or alone. He loved being with her, but he needed more alone time than he was getting. Probably because he was involved in his book. During his week off he'd be craving her attention while she worked.

She laughed. "I'm honestly surprised you want me around. I was certain you would want to be here alone pounding away at your computer while I was at work."

He sighed. "Of course I want you around. I think you're pretty amazing." He leaned forward and kissed her softly. "I'll try not to make you feel that way again." He needed to be better about showing her he wanted her around, whether he did or not. He knew his thoughts were unfair. He *did* want her there. He just didn't want to feel like he had to stop what he was doing for her.

"How fast do you type?" she asked.

He frowned at the quick change in subject. He would never understand the female mind. Never. "One hundred fifteen words per minute. Why?"

She blinked a few times. "I had no idea it was even possible to type that fast. When you were typing last night, it sounded like a machine gun, so I decided to ask you."

He shrugged. "I took typing in high school, and then again in college. My professor in college walked up behind me during the first day of class when I was typing a paper, and she said she was going to fail me on principle." He half-smiled at the memory of it.

"What principle is that? She couldn't just decide to fail someone the first day of class!" She was ready to go hunt down his teacher and tell him she was evil for even saying it.

He shook his head. "She was joking. She said it because I was already typing faster than she did."

Addie laughed. "Then why did you take the class? That's nuts!"

"I needed another elective, and it was an easy A. Was there nothing you took for an easy A?"

She grinned. "Yeah, I guess there were a couple of classes. Everyone does that." He was right. Everyone took electives that were easy for them. It was the way of the college world.

"What did you take because it was easy for you?"

"Me? I took an English history class from the Roman Empire to the Tudors. It was so much fun for me! I read the book before the class even started, and then I read it several more times too." She shrugged. "I still have it."

He looked at her as if she'd grown two heads. "Most people take easy stuff for their electives. What were you thinking?" He didn't hate history, but that sounded ridiculously complicated.

"I was thinking that all my classes were business, and I love history. What else?" She knew it was an odd choice for an elective, but she wasn't going to apologize for it.

"You're crazy, my dear wife."

She leaned forward and kissed him softly. "You have voices in your head that tell you what to write, and you call me crazy? Are you kidding me?" She'd never heard of a blacker pot calling a kettle black.

He pulled her onto his lap and kissed her, touching her through the thin fabric of her pajamas. "Are you sure you don't want to put your new nightgown on for me?" he asked, nibbling her ear with his teeth.

"Why? This isn't sexy enough for you?"

He laughed as he looked at her pajama shirt that proclaimed her the 'Queen of Everything.' "There are sexier things you could wear, but really? This works for me." His hand slid under the shirt and he stroked her breast. "Want me to demonstrate?"

"Isn't that what you're already doing?"

*****

Addie called Savannah the next morning on her way to work. She had nothing else to do on the forty-five minute subway ride. "He's going to make me crazy," she said as soon as the other woman answered.

Laughter came back to her over the line. "This must be Addie. Yeah, Jake is a special kind of snowflake. He can't figure out what day of the week it is half the time. If you need him to do something, tape a note to the corner of his computer, and set off five different alarms throughout the house. Scott said that's what he had to do when they were roommates in college and Jake was working on his first book. Now Scott just goes over there and gets his attention. Or he did before he moved to Manhattan, of course."

"Tell me what was hard about your marriage. You seem to be doing very well now." Savannah had made it clear at the reception something had happened when she first married Scott. Whatever that something was might help her deal with Jake.

Savannah sighed. "You know, Scott is a clueless man. He thought I should stay home and cook all day, because that's what his mother did."

"I hope you quickly disillusioned him of that!" Addie was glad Jake didn't have any of those misconceptions.

Savannah laughed. "We had a fight about it, but decided I would cook through the summer, but I'd go to work in the fall. I'm a teacher. Anyway, about a week later, he gave me a present. It was wrapped in Christmas paper and had thick dust on it. When I asked him who it was originally for, he said it was for his mother who had died a few years prior to that.

And when I opened it? It was a Kitchen Aid mixer. I would have gotten over it quickly if he hadn't told me the following morning that I must have PMS to be in such a bad mood."

Addie choked with laughter. "Oh, you have got to be kidding me! Yes, Scott is clueless all right. Jake isn't clueless, but he seems absent, if that makes sense. I mean, I understand becoming involved in work, but he's going way overboard." She wasn't certain how she would have reacted to being told she had PMS, but she might have set out to prove it.

"That's Jake. Give him a chance and use the alarm clock trick."

"Well, for today, I started a meal in the crock pot, so he wouldn't have to remember to get up and cook. He was supposed to start supper at seven yesterday evening, and didn't bother. I had it all ready in the fridge. He just had to pop it in the oven."

"And he forgot?"

"He never even heard me ask, even though he agreed to do it." That was the frustrating thing for Addie. If he hadn't agreed to do it, she'd have been fine with him not hearing her. But his agreement? That meant he was deliberately ignoring her.

Savannah sighed. "Yeah, you have to ask him to repeat what you said back to you, or he won't even know the conversation happened."

"That's what he told me," Addie said. "I think it's ridiculous, but I'll do it if it means he'll remember." She looked up and realized she was already at her stop. "All right, thanks for the chat. I won't kill him tonight."

"Good. Scott would be lost without him."

Addie smiled. "I'm getting off the subway and walking to the store now. We'll have to talk again soon." She could tell she was going to like Savannah just as soon as they had time to really get to know each other.

"If it gets too crazy, call Dr. Lachele. She gave me really good advice when I wanted to hurt Scott for his cluelessness."

"I will call her if I need to! Thanks again!" She ended the call and stuck her phone in her purse. She had a long day ahead of her, and she didn't need to be worrying about her husband. It was time to focus on her business.

*****

Their week went much smoother after that first

day. Jake did his best to go to bed when she did, but he would sneak out of bed in the middle of the night to get more work done. He was at the point where he needed to just finish this book so he could write the next one that was screaming at him. He wasn't so much money-driven as he was work-driven. He genuinely loved everything about his job, and it was hard for him to stop even though he knew he should.

Addie made breakfast every morning before she left for work, and he did his best to sit down with her to eat every evening, instead of eating at his computer while he wrote. He wondered if she knew what kind of sacrifice he was making? At least she worked six days per week, and he wouldn't have to worry about her always being there trying to talk to him when he needed to be working.

When she got home from work on Friday night, she sank down onto the couch and rubbed the back of her neck. It had been a really long week. She was used to sharing the cooking with her roommates, and now she was doing it all. It would have been nice if Jake had done more since he was the one home all day, and she was bringing in the bulk of their income, but watching him work, she could tell that he truly wasn't capable of doing more around the house than he did.

Once she got his attention she said, "Do you want to go out to dinner tonight? I didn't start anything before work."

He frowned. He really didn't want to take that much time away from his book, but he hadn't left the apartment since they got home on Sunday evening either. "Sure that would be fine. Where do you want to go?"

She shrugged. "We could just start walking and see what we see. Manhattan is so pretty at night."

He hated the idea of being gone that long, but he reluctantly agreed. He still felt like he owed her for the incident on Monday. "We can do that." He looked down at himself. "Let me get a shower first?"

She nodded. "Sounds good. This is a new area of the city for me, and I don't know it as well, so I'll just see what I can find close to here."

Once he was in the shower, she pulled out her phone and frowned at the small screen. It would be easier if she just used his computer. She could get her laptop out, but why? His was right there.

The words he was writing caught her eye immediately. "*The Sorcerers of Mythria!* He's my favorite writer! I married Roger Holiday. Holy moly!" As soon as the words crossed her lips, she was angry. He'd acted as if he made a pittance from his work, but she'd seen articles talking about the million dollar deal he'd gotten for his last book. *The*

Sorcerers of Mythria was one of the most popular series in Science Fiction. Why would he lie to her?

She moved back to the couch, and did the search on her phone, leaving his computer the way she'd found it. She thought about confronting him, but decided instead to ask him questions about his work, and see how much he'd tell her. He must have seen his books on her shelf and known she was a fan. She felt like an idiot. She'd married her favorite writer and had no clue.

She did her quick search and found a small restaurant not far from the apartment with good ratings and decent prices. Not that she needed to worry about prices when she was married to Roger Holiday. What had he been thinking hiding his true identity from her?

She had herself under control before he emerged from the bathroom with a towel wrapped around his waist. He was fresh shaven and looked good to her. Not so good that she didn't still want to slap him, though. She worked hard to keep her face impassive. She couldn't show how angry she was until she was ready to confront him.

"Do I need a suit for this place? Or jeans?"

"Slacks and a nice shirt is good," she answered automatically. "I'm just wearing my work clothes." She wore a pair of slacks and a nice blouse, but nothing terribly fancy.

He nodded and disappeared into the bedroom, coming out a few minutes later, ready to go. "Did you make reservations?

"No, they don't take them at this place." When they left the apartment, she locked the door. "Did I give you a key yet?" She had two, but one might still be in her jewelry box.

He shook his head. "Not yet. I haven't gone anywhere on my own. I'm sure I will eventually." Like as soon as he finished his book. He was going to go and get her the biggest bouquet of flowers she'd ever seen, just to thank her for putting up with him while he wrote. And keeping him fed. That was a big deal as well.

He took her hand as they walked through the busy streets. "The restaurant is only about three blocks away, so it's not far. I hope you like Italian." She really didn't care if he liked the food or not. At that point he'd better eat it and do it with a smile. She wouldn't be responsible for her actions otherwise.

"I love Italian. I really love New York Italian, because it seems so authentic." Now that he was out of the apartment, he was thrilled to be out looking at all the people. Every person he met ended up in a book somehow. It wasn't usually a whole person, more just a piece of every person.

"It's usually very authentic. Often the cook will come out and yell at the servers in Italian. It's fun to watch." She stopped walking. "Here it is."

They went into the small restaurant and were seated quickly. She picked up her menu. She'd wait to start their discussion until after they had ordered. "It's not a good sign that there was no wait on a Friday night," she said, a bit worried about her choice.

He shrugged. "We're eating late. It's after eight-thirty. I'm sure everyone is off doing other things by now."

"Do you mind eating so late?" she asked, glancing at him over the top of her menu. Not that they had a choice. The store didn't close until six, and she didn't make it home until seven. If they wanted to eat out, they had to do it late.

"Oh not at all. I enjoy eating any time I remember to."

She read over the menu selections and closed her menu, waiting patiently for him to do the same. When he set his menu down, he reached across the table and took her hand. "Tell me about the book you're writing," she urged.

He shrugged. "Oh, it's just a boring science fiction book. Dragons and princesses in a far-away land. Nothing to write home about." He chose his words carefully, not wanting to give away his identity. He had seen his books on the shelf in her room, so he knew she was a fan. Unsure of why he didn't want her to know yet, he assumed it was just because he enjoyed the illusion of having a wife who cared about him because she liked him. Not because of money. Of course, he knew he should have already told her, and he would soon. When he figured out how.

"Really? Sounds fascinating! What will you call it?" She leaned forward in her chair as she asked, making sure he knew she was extremely interested.

"I haven't decided yet."

"Really?" she asked. "I'd heard that the next Roger Holiday book would be called *Dancing With Dragons*. Did I read wrong?"

His eyes widened, and he frowned. "How'd you find out?"

"Does it really matter? It was easy to put two and two together and add up to the fact that my husband is a lying pig."

The waiter stopped at their table, looking back and forth between them as if he'd heard what Addie had said. "Can I get you some drinks?" he asked, looking like he was almost afraid to interrupt the conversation.

"I'll have a Sprite, please," she said sweetly, not looking at Jake.

"Coke."

The waiter nodded. "I'll be right back with your drinks and to get your order." He hurried away, obviously not wanting to be any part of the conversation taking place.

"Addie, you have to believe me. I never meant to hide it from you, but when women discover that I'm Roger Holiday, they all go insane and immediately profess undying love for me. I wanted you to get a chance to know me, Jake, and not be worried about how much money I make or what kind of books I write."

She shook her head. "And did I pass your test? Am I good enough to be married to the great Roger Holiday?"

He sighed. "Please don't be angry with me."

"How could I not be angry with you? Every single book you've ever written is on my shelf at home. You knew I was a fan, and you never said anything. Our whole marriage is built on a lie!"

"I never meant to lie to you!" He hadn't been thinking about how she'd feel about his deception.

He'd only been worried about making certain her feelings were real.

She shrugged. "A meaningful lie and a lie by omission result in the same thing. They're both lies."

He shook his head. "I just wanted you to have a chance to get to know me, Jake. It's hard for everyone I meet to know I'm Roger Holiday, and expect me to act accordingly." He closed his eyes for a moment, worried this was something she wouldn't be able to forgive him for. It had never really occurred to him just how angry she'd get. "I'm really sorry I deceived you. Can you forgive me?"

"I honestly don't know. You're my husband, the man I'm supposed to spend the rest of my life with, and I've just found out you lied to me for the first two weeks of our marriage. It's a hard pill to swallow." She'd been raised to always forgive. God forgave all of her sins. And she probably could forgive. But could she trust again?

"I'll do whatever I can to make it up to you. I swear." His eyes pled with her to understand.

She sighed. "It's not about making it up to me. It's about whether or not I can trust you again." She eyed him skeptically. "Is there anything else you're not telling me?"

"I can contribute a lot more than two thousand a

month to our living expenses," he said with a half-grin, knowing that would be good news and not bad. "Um...I have a house in Montana that I'm not sure if I'll sell. My parents deeded it to me when I graduated from college."

"Is that all?"

"I don't get a discount at my friend's place in South Dakota. He expects me to pay full price." He racked his brain for anything else that he could have lied about, either by omission or on purpose. "I think that's all. If I can think of anything else you need to know, I'll tell you right away."

She sighed. "Where do we go from here?"

He shrugged. "You tell me. I need to finish my book I'm working on, but it'll be done soon. After that, I'll take a week off, and we'll have some extra time together. Does that work?"

"I guess." She didn't know how to explain how hurt she felt about his deceit. Especially when the fan girl inside her was dancing with joy. She was married to her favorite writer. "I rearranged my schedule so I'll have Saturdays and Sundays off from now on. I'll get the laundry and everything done during the day on Saturdays. Can you spend Saturday evenings with me?"

He nodded slowly. He wanted to spend time

with her, so he would. He might have to get up in the middle of the night to write, but that would be nothing new for him. His schedules were never what anyone would call normal anyway. "I can make that happen." He took her hand and brought it to his lips. "Thank you for giving me another chance."

She nodded briefly. She wasn't certain she was giving him another chance so much as doing what she promised to do in the contract. But she wouldn't break the contract. Before she could say that, their food arrived.

She'd work at forgiving him, of course, but trusting? That would be a long time coming.

Chapter Six

Addie spent Saturday doing all the chores that had been put off during the week. Now that she realized they had more money to work with, she would set up laundry pickup and delivery for the following week, but it was just too late to mess with it. She spent the morning in a laundromat around the corner from the apartment, reading one of her husband's books. It was strange to realize that they were his as she read, but she was starting to like the idea.

The stories that she loved had been created in the mind of the man she'd married. When she looked at him, she saw him differently. Maybe that was why he hadn't told her. Maybe he didn't want her to see him differently.

When she got home, he was still tapping away at his keyboard, which was no surprise. She was starting to think the man wasn't happy unless his fingers were typing away at something. She put the laundry away, and then pulled out her laptop to order their groceries for the week. She cleaned the bathroom while waiting for the groceries, and when the groceries arrived, she put them away, made sandwiches for both of them, putting his beside him on the desk, and started dinner in the crock pot.

She cleaned the entire apartment around him, and he only spoke to her when he got up to go to the bathroom. She was amazed that he could be so focused on something that nothing seemed able to penetrate the mental walls he built up around himself. She wasn't certain if his intense focus made him admirable or just plain annoying. Either way, he was hers for the long haul. She didn't believe in divorce.

*****

Addie enjoyed introducing Jake around at church on Sunday. Part of her wanted to scream that he was the famous science fiction writer, Roger Holiday, but most of her recognized that would make him uncomfortable. He was simply Jake, her husband.

No one had known she was getting married, because she hadn't wanted to have a huge number of people at her wedding. With three sisters and three brothers, and their families, the wedding had been big enough already. Matchrimony had brought in the preacher who married them, so she even had to introduce him to her pastor and his wife, both of whom were very welcoming of him.

They took a cab to her parents' house afterward. She told him she didn't mind taking the subway, but he shook his head. "No point working as hard as I do to take the subway. We'll take a cab."

Addie wondered if she'd ever be able to just casually spend more money than she needed to on something, just because she had it, but the answer was clear to her: she would. She really already had by setting up laundry services. She certainly was able to spend hours every Saturday morning working on their laundry, but why bother? She could throw a little money at it, and avoid the task, doing something she enjoyed for a change.

When they arrived at her parents' house in Brooklyn, she wished she could make everything magically right between her and Jake, if only for a few hours. Her parents would notice something wasn't right between them. She didn't want to deceive them, but even worse was the idea that they would realize something was amiss. In this case, deception was the only real answer.

She stopped on the sidewalk leading up to the house and looked at Jake. "My parents need to think everything is perfect between us. I really don't want them to worry."

"I wish we could skip straight past making your parents think everything is perfect to everything *being* perfect again. I'll do my best, though."

"Thanks." She said nothing in response to his wish as they walked up to the house. He'd chosen his path. She'd try, but it was hard to regain trust. If she could do it, she'd snap her fingers and make it happen, but she knew that would never work. Nothing she could think of would.

Her father stepped outside as they reached the front door. "I was starting to wonder if you two were going to stand out here talking all day."

Addie walked into her father's arms, hugging him tightly. She rested her head on his broad shoulder, wishing for a moment he could make everything better for her. She wanted to cry, but she kept a smile on her face as she pulled away. "So good to see you, Dad."

Billy Myers eyed his youngest child. "You happy?"

She nodded. "Jake's a good man." And she knew he was. She just...didn't trust him any longer. "I'm going to run in and say 'hi' to mom." She passed her father, unable to withstand his scrutiny for another minute as she hurried to the kitchen. "Is there anything I can do to help?"

Her mother spun around from the sink, where she was peeling potatoes. "Well, look who the cat dragged in!" Carolyn's eyes went up and down her youngest daughter. "I guess he didn't kill you after all."

Addie had to laugh at that. "Did you really think he would?" Surely her mother had known she was just being silly about that.

"Well, how was I supposed to know? I'd never met the man, and neither had you!"

"Why don't I finish peeling the potatoes? I know that's hard on your back. You take a break." It was a smooth change of subject, but more than that? It was the truth. Her mother had injured her back long before Addie was born, and she'd grown up doing her best to keep her mother from doing anything that would make her hurt more than she had to.

Carolyn gladly stepped away from the hated chore. "I'll set the table. How was that place in South Dakota? Was it nice?" She got down plates and glasses as she talked.

"Oh, it was really amazing." While Addie peeled the potatoes, she described the resort and the way they'd kept it preserved. "It was really like stepping back in time. I'd love to go again sometime if I get the chance. I can't imagine anything that would make me feel like I was back in the time period more than that did."

"Sounds like an interesting place to visit. Maybe I can talk your father into taking me there for our forty-fifth anniversary. I wouldn't mind trying the 'healing waters' for the arthritis in my knees. Or my back either for that matter."

Knowing her mother had always been one to go for natural remedies over traditional medicine, Addie wasn't surprised at all. "I don't know if there will be any real healing benefits, but I know you'll enjoy it."

Carolyn smiled. "I'm sure I'll enjoy it. Any time spent with your father is good time."

From anyone else the words would have sounded false to Addie, but she knew her mother meant them. Her parents got on each others' nerves at times, but they always loved and stood by each other. "I don't have any idea what it costs. Jake paid for it."

Carolyn eyed her daughter. "He should have paid for it. Are you two having money issues?"

"Not in the way you mean. We have plenty." Addie swore to herself she wouldn't say another word. She didn't want her mother to know how her husband had deceived her.

"Oh. I thought he was a writer," Carolyn said with surprise.

Was her mother where she got the notion that writers were all struggling and none of them could support themselves? "He is. He's a famous science fiction writer. He's my favorite writer actually."

Addie tried to sound like it was every day a girl married her favorite writer.

"I had no idea! I won't worry so much about him murdering you then."

"Do you think famous people can't be murderers? I'm not sure why you think that way, Mom. Look at Phil Spector. He killed his wife. He was famous."

Carolyn frowned at Addie. "Are you trying to make me worry more?"

"No, I'm not. I just don't think you should believe someone is good just because they're famous. Not everyone famous is good, just like not everyone who's not famous is bad." Her mother's ideas about life amazed Addie at times.

"But there's less of a chance he'll kill you. Isn't there?"

"He's not going to kill me. Don't worry about that so much." Addie shook her head at her mother as she put the potatoes on the stove. "What else can I do?"

"Get the pot roast out of the oven and whip up some gravy." Carolyn walked to the table and sat down. "I need to sit for a few minutes." Her back issues made it so she couldn't be in any position for long.

Addie grabbed some oven mitts, removed the roast, and started the process of making gravy. "Has Dad talked any more about doing consulting work for the city?"

"He's decided against it. He likes not having to wake up to the alarm clock for a change, and he decided he doesn't want to give that up."

"I can understand that." Addie hated mornings herself, but they were a necessary evil.

"Heather's having a baby." Heather was Addie's second oldest sister. "They're really hoping for a girl this time."

Addie smiled. "After four boys, I would expect so. Why else would they be having a fifth?"

"Your sister loves being a stay at home mom, just like I was. Do you think there's any chance you'll stay home once children start coming?" Carolyn didn't think women should work once the babies started coming. She thought it was fine and dandy to have a career, but not if you had children. Everything should be given up at that point.

Addie shook her head. "No chance at all. I have a store to run. I love what I do. There's no need for me to stay home." How many times did she have to explain it to her mother? She was choosing a career. Yes, she'd have a family when she was ready, but that didn't mean she had to stay home with the children.

"Will Jake take care of the baby while you're at work?"

"I think we'll probably just hire a nanny, but we're not even planning on thinking about it yet. Not for at least a year." Addie knew her mother wanted more grandkids, but she had fifteen and two more on the way. She could wait. "Gravy's done. Do you want the potatoes mashed?"

"Yeah, go ahead and mash them, please."

As soon as she was finished, Addie put a big bowl of mashed potatoes on the table. She added the gravy, meat, and carrots. She filled glasses for everyone before calling the two men to eat. "I hope you're hungry. Mom cooked enough to feed an army."

Billy and Jake seemed to be engrossed in conversation. "We're coming!" Billy looked at Jake. "My wife is going to make me eat this as leftovers for a week if you don't eat a lot and rave about it. Then she'll send some home with you. I don't care if you throw it away, just don't make me eat it forever."

"Yes, sir." Jake winked at Addie. "I'm going to rescue your father from the leftovers," he whispered.

Addie shook her head. "Mom's going to figure it out, and then you'll be on her poop list too!"

Jakes eyes twinkled as he asked, "Poop list? Really?"

She shrugged. "You know what I mean. I don't use those words, and I especially don't use them in my mama's house."

He chuckled, putting a hand to the small of her back. She wanted to push it away, because she was still annoyed with him, but she didn't want her parents to know there was anything wrong between them.

When they were all seated, her father said a prayer for them. When Jake's hand found hers under the table, she didn't push him away. Instead she held tightly to his hand for the prayer.

"How're things going at the store, Addie?" Billy asked as he served himself a huge portion of the mashed potatoes.

"Oh, really well. Bailey did fine while I was gone. No mistakes that I can find, and she didn't have to call me even once." She took a bite of her roast. "Mom, this roast is great." She had always loved her mother's cooking, and this meal was no exception.

"Thanks! It's your dad's favorite!"

Billy looked at Jake with pleading eyes. Jake took the hint. "This is wonderful, Mrs. Myers. I wish Addie had more time to cook this way." Truly, he was more than satisfied with the food Addie cooked for him. She provided much better than frozen pizza, which was about all he ever fed himself.

Carolyn gave Addie a look. "I was just telling her she should plan on staying home once you start having children."

Jake wiped his mouth with a napkin. With as angry as Addie still was, he wasn't sure they'd ever be able to have children, because she may never let him touch her again. "I think if and when children arrive, we'll probably get a full time nanny. I can't take time off work to care for a baby, and I know Addie cares more about her store than that."

Carolyn frowned. "You're not even planning to raise your own child? I raised you better than that, Addie!"

Obviously her mother thought shaming her in front of her new husband would make her change her mind. "Yes, you did. But you also raised me to be strong and think for myself. I know what I want, and I want to keep running my store. It makes me happy."

"Children would make you happier!"

Jake looked back and forth between mother and daughter. "Addie has the right to choose her own path, Mrs. Myers. You can't expect her to do everything you did, simply because you did it that way."

"Well, I never!" Carolyn looked more than a little offended by her son-in-law's words.

Billy sighed. "Carolyn? Let it go. She has the right to be a store owner or a stay at home mom. She also has the right to take up featherweight boxing if she wants to. We raised her right, and now she gets to make her own decisions."

Carolyn obviously didn't like her husband's answer, but she didn't say anything else. Addie was relieved. Her mother usually went on and on about how she was doing things wrong, but this time she'd had two defenders.

"The food really is wonderful, Mrs. Myers," Jake said again. "Would you mind if we took a bit of it home for lunches this week?" He knew he was being obvious, but maybe she wouldn't say anything. He certainly didn't want to be on her 'poop list' as Addie so eloquently put it.

Carolyn shook her head. "Of course not." She never had been, nor would she ever be a woman who turned down a guest in her home.

Billy winked at Jake and mouthed the words, "Thank you."

Jake pretended not to see it as he continued eating.

Once lunch was over, Jake stood. "We should go," he said.

"Can we take ten minutes for me to help Mom with the dishes?" Addie asked. She knew Jake was in a hurry to get back to work, but she really didn't want to upset her mother by just taking off either. In her mother's house all the women helped with the cooking, and all the women helped with the dishes. As a child she'd often protested that the boys should help too, but it had gotten her nowhere, so she'd just learned to accept it as her lot in life.

Jake nodded reluctantly. "But then I've got to get back to work."

"I'll be ready after the dishes." Addie got to her feet and hurried around the kitchen, gathering dishes and putting them into the sink to rinse and get into the dishwasher.

Carolyn got to her feet, helping her daughter. "You aren't spending your Sunday off together?" she asked with a frown.

"We spent half the day together. He'll work the other half. I've got some paperwork to do for the store. We're a good team, because we both work so hard." Addie knew it was true. Lachele had picked a good man for her. She would have gone crazy being married to Scott.

Carolyn shook her head. "I really don't know how you do it. You're newlyweds. You should be spending every moment you can together."

Addie agreed with her mother, so she said nothing. They needed more time together, but they weren't going to get it. "He takes a week off every month, and we'll have more time together then. I may arrange my schedule to do the same. Or at least plan a couple of days off during his week off."

"I guess if he wants to keep making the kind of money he does, he needs to work that hard."

Addie frowned. "You know that sounds like he's incredibly money-driven, and I just don't think that's the case. I think he loves his work so much that he's just driven to do it. He needs to work like other people need air. I've never seen anything like it."

Carolyn frowned. "You really believe that?"

"I really do!"

*****

As soon as they arrived home, Jake returned to his computer, immediately going back to work. Addie stowed the leftovers in the refrigerator. She'd serve them for dinner the next night. There really was enough for a couple of more meals, and her mother had halved the leftovers with her. Addie shook her head. Someday her mother would learn that she was no longer cooking for a family of nine!

She settled on the couch with her laptop and went through the weekly reports for the store, making the orders that needed to be made. After a while, she glanced up and saw Jake watching her. "Is everything all right?"

He got up and moved to the couch beside her, his arm going around her shoulders. He waited for her to flinch away, but when she didn't, he pulled her close. "Do you have a lot more work to do?"

She shook her head. "I'm just finishing up. Why?"

He took the computer from her lap and placed it on the small coffee table. "I just want to talk for a minute, if you don't mind."

"Not at all." Why was he paying attention to her instead of his computer? "What's up?"

"Well, first, I just want to say I'm sorry one more time. After spending two days with you, I knew you cared for me even without knowing about the money I made. Telling you before we came home would have been ideal. I shouldn't have waited."

She nodded. "Thank you for saying that. I've felt like you didn't think you could trust me, even after the honeymoon, when I feel like I told you everything."

He sighed, pulling her closer and kissing her forehead. "Not at all. I'm sorry I made you feel that way."

"I forgive you." For the first time since she'd discovered who he really was, she felt like she could move on past it. He was saying all the right things. She believed he really meant them.

"I also wanted to talk about this apartment. Did you sign a long lease?"

"No, I just subleased for two months from a friend. I didn't know where we'd end up, and I didn't feel like I had the right to make the decision for us, but Dr. Lachele had given me the impression we'd be living here in Manhattan. So I figured I needed to find us a spot. We couldn't keep living with my three roommates, especially since I shared a room with Danielle!"

"Well, this place is pretty small. Would you be willing to look at larger places on my next week off? I'd love to have an office to write in. Then I wouldn't feel like I'm taking up the whole living room. You'd feel like you could make a little more noise, I'm sure." He watched her carefully for a response.

She nodded. "I think that's a really good idea. We could get a two or even three bedroom place. Do you want to keep living in an apartment or try to find a house?"

"An apartment for now, I think. Neither of us has time to think about maintaining a lawn or anything." He turned to her more fully on the couch. "I hope you didn't mind leaving your parents so quickly. I had this idea for a way I could fix the last scene of my book."

"You finished? Really?"

He nodded. "Well, I still have to edit it, and I'll add several thousand more words in edits, but I finished the first draft, which for me is the hardest part."

"You edit your own book? Don't you have an editor?" It didn't make sense to her that he would have to go through the slow process of editing his own work when she knew he must have someone who was paid to do it.

"I do have an editor, but I still edit my own book first. I tend to skimp on details in the first draft, and then I go back and add them." He shrugged. "I'll spend the next week or so in edits, and then I'll be done with this one."

"Will you take some time off when you're done?"

He nodded. "Yeah, I take at least a week off between books. I need to go back to Montana and get the rest of my stuff from my house there. I'll leave the furniture, but I need my books and stuff. Which is another reason why we need a bigger place. I need room for my books!"

She laughed. "Sounds to me like you might need a Kindle!"

"Don't we all?" He cupped her face in his hands, leaning over to kiss her softly. "I'm so happy to hear you laugh again. I thought I'd blown it for us."

"I wasn't sure." She looked straight into his eyes. "I was really hurt, but I don't want our relationship to be over. Do you want me to take a couple of days off work and go to Montana with you? We could always shop for apartments when we were done."

"Would you mind? I'd love for you to get to know Scott and Savannah better. And Kaeden too, I guess, but right now? He just poops a lot."

She giggled. "Most babies do. I would love to go with you."

He leaned over and kissed her again, this time more passionately. His arms wrapped around her and he pulled her close. "Wanna know what I'd love to do?"

"What?"

He stood and helped her to her feet, keeping her hand in his as he headed to the bedroom. He pulled off his shirt and sat on the bed, facing her. She stood in front of him. "I'll give you three guesses." His hands went to her shirt, and he started unbuttoning it before pushing it off her shoulders.

"You're tired and want to take a nap?" she said, with a twinkle in her eye.

"No. Two more tries." His unzipped her slacks and pushed them down off her hips.

"You want to read in bed naked? I'd let you read your book to me!" That sounded like a terrific idea to her.

"One more guess!" He unclasped her bra and dropped it to the floor.

"Um...You want to draw smiley faces on my belly?"

"Nope. Wrong three times. Now you have to pay the penalty!"

She frowned. "Oh no. What could that penalty be?"

"Why don't I show you?" He pulled her down onto the bed with him.

Chapter Seven

Addie started to live for the day Jake's edits were done. Always she'd lived for her store, but she found she craved his attention. He finished the edits on Friday the following week, so Addie arranged to take the following week off for their trip to Montana and apartment hunting. They'd already been married four weeks when they got on the plane to pack up his things.

When they landed, Scott and Savannah were waiting at the airport with Kaeden sleeping in his car seat at the back of the SUV. Jake climbed into the back seat and let Addie sit in the middle with Kaeden. "You staying at your old house, Jake?" Scott asked.

"Yeah. We have too much to get done to do anything else." Jake sighed. "This isn't just a fun trip." He wished it was though. He wished they were staying with Scott and Savannah, so the two women could get to know one another better. It would be nice if they were as close as he and Scott were.

Savannah turned and looked at Addie. "Do you want to come to supper tonight? Or do you want us to go to a grocery store so you'll have food there?

You'll be surprised at the lack of delivery places here."

Addie smiled. "I know New Yorkers are blessed with more delivery places than the rest of the country. I don't mind cooking, but I'd love to come over as well. It would be nice to get to know you and Scott better." She loved what she knew of Savannah.

"Well, why don't we drop you off to get started? We took Scott's truck to Jake's house, so you'll have something to drive while you're here."

"Thanks for that," Jake said. "We could have rented a car, but this makes it a bit easier. We won't have to take load after load of boxes to be shipped. We can just do it all in one or two trips with the truck."

"My truck is your truck. You wreck it? You buy me a new one. Heck, just wreck it toward the end of your time here. I need a new truck anyway." Because they were sitting at a stoplight, Scott looked in the rearview mirror at his friend to see his reaction.

"I'll buy you an old beat up truck!" Jake told him. "Maybe I can find one like you drove in high school."

Scott laughed. "Oh yeah, that would be awesome. Remember that time we were driving up and down drag and my truck died, and you had to get out and push?"

Jake rolled his eyes. "I was trying to flirt with girls out the window, and the next thing I knew they were at the next light, and we were still sitting there like a couple of morons." He'd been mortified at the time, but he had no problem laughing about it now.

Addie looked at Jake. "You were flirting with girls?" She tried to sound angry with him, but she couldn't help but smile at the picture of the two men stranded while the girls went on.

"Don't worry, baby. We were barely sixteen, so you'd have been about nine. It doesn't count if you were pre-pubescent." Jake winked at her.

Savannah turned around from the front seat and looked at Addie. "Scott uses that line with me, too. We'll show them differently later."

Addie grinned. She and Savanna had spoken on the phone several times, and she was happy to be able to call the other woman a friend. She looked forward to having some face to face time with her, and not just phone, texts, and internet. Sometimes you just needed to be able to touch someone.

"We're really thankful you're willing to cook tonight. It'll save me from having to spend the time. I think we're going to be way too busy to think about eating. Jake says there's only one restaurant to speak of in town." It was mind boggling to Addie to think about actually living in a place that had so little, but she guessed she could see the appeal of a small town. It would be nice to occasionally run into people she knew around town.

Savannah nodded. "The diner. There's this waitress who acts like she owns the guys. I think they dated every female within a two hundred mile radius." She made a face. "I went for an in-service training, and the teacher I was taking over for? Her sister dated Scott, but she didn't. I couldn't believe he'd actually missed a girl in the state of Montana!"

Addie looked at Jake. "Did you have the same number of girls hanging off you as Scott did?"

Jake shook his head. "It was harder to get girls when you were on the tennis team and in the chess club. Scott was a football player."

"Oh, well, I only liked football players if they were in the chess club too. I was a nerd in high school. I wanted to date the guy who would have a job someday and not a concussion," Addie told them.

Savannah laughed. "Dr. Lachele really does know what she's doing! Being married to Jake would make me crazy, and I sure couldn't see you giving up your store for Scott. Or him being willing to let you run it instead of being home to cook his dinner every night."

"I'm still reserving judgment," Addie said with a

grin.

"Hey, you've made it through a month, and you're sitting in a car with each other without wanting to kill anyone. That's pretty impressive!" Scott interjected from the front.

"We've never tried to kill each other!" Jake said proudly. He really did feel like it was an accomplishment.

"We never tried, but I did think about breaking a vase over his head a few times," Savannah said.

Addie suppressed a giggle. "Did he deserve it?" She was sure he had, but it would be nice to hear Scott's side of things.

"Oh, more than!" Scott answered. "She's a saint for putting up with me!"

"Well, I wasn't perfect either. No one is." Savannah smiled at Scott. "Now that we're through the first year, I think we're going to be just fine."

"Until I do something so stupid you want to hit me over the head with a vase again?"

Jake shook his head. "Well, stop doing stupid things then! Oh, wait...forgot who I'm talking to!"

"Jake?" Scott asked.

"Yeah?"

"You're a freak."

"Oh, I wish I had a best friend like that," Addie said to Savannah. "I can just feel the love."

"Wouldn't it be wonderful if we all could?" Savannah asked.

*****

Addie wasn't certain what she expected when they pulled up to Scott and Savannah's home a few hours later, but it wasn't the big old ranch house that stood proudly in the middle of several outbuildings. It was pretty, in an old-fashioned rustic kind of way, but it was surprising to Addie, who loved New York with everything inside her, that another girl from Manhattan could be so happy in Montana.

Once they were inside, Savannah gave Addie a quick tour of the house. "This house is certainly full of history," Addie said.

Savannah laughed. "Yeah, it's old, but I think it's such a beautiful place. I've only been here for a year, but already I couldn't imagine living anywhere else. Scott's great-grandfather built it."

"It's a wonderful place to raise children," Addie

said honestly.

"Do you still think you'll put off having children until you've been married for a year?"

"Oh, at least. I put in a lot of hours in my store, and Jake's so involved in his writing. I can just see leaving him home alone with a baby, and him not even noticing that the baby cried." Addie sighed. "He sure is good at tuning out the world around him. I'm sure it's a skill he needed to learn, but it's crazy."

"You'll need to hire a nanny if you want to keep working. Jake will never be able to do his share." Savannah opened the door to the baby's room. "He's a good man, but he sure doesn't notice the world around him."

Addie sighed as she looked at the walls. "This is beautiful! Did you quilt this yourself?" she asked, referring to a Sesame Street wall hanging.

"Dr. Lachele did. She said she's going to make something special for each of her Matchrimony munchkins." Savannah laughed. "At first she kept calling Kaeden her first Matchrimony grandbaby, and then she decided Matchrimony munchkins has a better ring to it. She's never gone back."

"I haven't had to call Dr. Lachele yet. We had a hard time for a little while, but we worked through it." Addie prided herself on not needing the counselor's help. They were doing just fine by themselves.

Savannah raised an eyebrow. "You will. Trust me. She's free for your first year. You might as well take advantage."

"We really haven't needed her." Addie hadn't told anyone about the way Jake had deceived her about his success as a writer, and she didn't plan to start with Savannah. They'd worked through it, and that was really all that mattered.

"Have you guys said the 'L' word yet?"

Addie shook her head. "We've only been married a month. I'm not ready to say it or hear it!" Sure, she enjoyed their time together. She loved the sex. But love? She was a long way from love!

"You really believe that?" Savannah asked. "If Jake said he loved you, you'd reject it?"

"Well, no, but I don't know how I'd respond. I mean, he's a great guy, and I like being around him. He's a good husband to me, but that doesn't mean I love him." Addie shrugged. "I'd probably say, 'Thank you.'"

"Do you resent the time he spends at the computer?"

"Just a little," Addie responded. "I work a lot of

hours as well."

"Do you live for your days off together?"

"That doesn't mean anything!" Addie protested.

"You love him. I'd be willing to bet he loves you too, but just hasn't said it yet." Savannah closed the door to Kaeden's room and headed back down the stairs. "Is Jake going to sell his parents' house? You guys would always be welcome to stay here when you come to visit."

"I'm really not sure." Addie was almost offended that she knew so little about her husband.

"Oh yeah. His parents are traveling throughout the country in their RV. They have been since Jake finished college. It was always their dream, but they wanted him to have stability as he was finishing college. He graduated, and they were gone the next week." Savannah led the way back to the kitchen. "I made bison steaks, baked potatoes, and salad. I hope that's all right."

Addie saw the table was already set even as she wrinkled her nose. "Bison steaks? Why would you make bison steaks?" She didn't even realize there were still buffalo. She thought they were extinct.

"Because bison are the only cattle indigenous to the United States, they have less fat than beef, don't need to be vaccinated, and have a better taste. Why wouldn't you eat bison?" Scott asked from behind her. His arms were crossed over his chest as if he were preparing for a fight. He was obviously passionate about the subject.

Jake laughed and walked over, putting his arm around Addie's shoulders. "Stop the lecture, Scott. She didn't know you were a bison rancher."

Scott looked at Jake incredulously. "You didn't tell her? Why wouldn't you say something?"

"Look, man, I know you think being a bison rancher is your identity, and there's nothing else to you, but I just never mentioned what you did other than ranching. I didn't dwell on that. We've only been married a month. I had your life story planned for sometime in the third month." He winked at Addie who grinned up at him.

Scott shook his head. "We don't eat beef. Only bison. Even Jake eats only bison meat, right Jake?"

Addie looked at Jake, wondering how he'd respond to that. For the month she'd known him, he'd eaten a lot of beef. "Right, Jake?" she echoed.

Jake grinned. "Scott? It's not easy to find bison meat in other parts of the country. I've been eating beef like it's going out of style." He didn't feel bad about it either. If bison had been readily available, then yes, he'd have chosen it over beef if only to support his friend. But it wasn't, so he hadn't.

Scott looked at Jake as if he'd grown two heads. "Are you kidding me? I feel so betrayed!" He shook his head. "And beef is out of style! It has been for years!"

Jake laughed. "I'd stay on my no beef fast if I could find bison elsewhere. You can't really expect me to give up red meat, though. I don't know if I could!" He knew his friend had spent very little time outside of the area of Montana where he'd been born and raised. He honestly probably didn't know how hard it was to obtain in other places.

Scott shook his head. "You could if you wanted to."

Addie decided to help her husband out. "I'm the one who buys the food, and he eats whatever I cook. I didn't know about the bison meat thing, so really? It's my fault!" She wasn't certain why eating bison meat was so important to Scott, but she'd do it, or at least tell him she'd do it, if he'd be quiet about it.

"I guess I can forgive you, since you didn't know. You'll make sure you buy Montana bison meat from now on instead of beef, though, right?" Scott asked. He gave her a look that told her she needed to agree or get out of his house.

Addie shrugged. "I'll do my best. It never

occurred to me to even look to see if my supermarket carried bison. The next time I shop, I'll see if that's on the website."

Savannah sighed. "I miss shopping for my groceries online and having them delivered. It's hard to take the baby to the grocery store. I've started going on Saturdays so Scott can watch the baby. Of course, since I'm nursing and he won't take a bottle, that means that I have to make sure he eats right before I leave."

Scott shrugged. "Raising our child without the pollution of New York in a close knit community is worth the trade-off though, right?"

"I think so whenever I'm not grocery shopping," Savannah replied. She opened the oven and removed the baked potatoes, leaving them atop the stove in their foil wraps. "I'm going to get the steaks from the grill, and I'll be right back." She took a platter from the counter and went out to get the steaks, coming back in less than three minutes later. "Are we ready to eat?"

"I am. Packing is hard work," Addie responded. "I'm starving."

The table was already set with iced tea at every setting. "I'll help with the dishes," Addie told Savannah once they were all seated.

"No, you can't. You're my guest." Savannah passed a bowl with the potatoes, still in their foil, to Addie. "I couldn't let you help."

Addie laughed. "In the house I grew up in, you help with dishes, or you go hungry. Well, the girls had to help at least. The boys were above that." She rolled her eyes, letting her friend know what she thought of the gender inequality in her parents' home.

Savannah shook her head. "Kaeden is going to know how to do dishes!"

"All men should know how." Addie added butter and cheese to her baked potato.

"I agree." Savannah glared at Scott as if she wanted him to argue with her about it.

Scott wisely stayed silent.

Chapter Eight

Sorting through everything in someone else's house was strange for Addie. She found photo albums full of pictures of Jake as a child. She couldn't help but sit down to look through them. When Jake came into the room from packing the garage, he found her curled up on his sofa, flipping through the pages, a smile lighting up her face.

"What did you find?" he asked, moving to sit beside her on the couch. When he saw the pictures in the album, he became entranced. So many memories were packed away in the big book.

She moved the album so it was half on his lap and half on hers. "Do you know who that baby girl you're playing with in all these pictures is?" It seemed as if three fourths of the pictures had another baby in them, and the two were side by side in carriers or standing in just diapers playing with toys. So far she'd seen about two years worth of pictures of the two of them.

Jake squinted at the album. "Baby girl? That's Scott. Our mothers were best friends, so he was my first playmate. He's two months older than me." He started chuckling.

"He looks like a girl, but don't tell him I said that! Look at those blond curls! He looked just like Kaeden does. Or I guess Kaeden looks just like he did. Either way." The resemblance between father and son was strong. Of course, Savannah and Scott had very similar coloring, so she was certain that added to it.

Jake laughed. "Yeah, he looked like a girl until his dad forced his mom to cut his hair for the first time. It was so curly and pretty. His mother didn't want to cut it." He shrugged. "I still tease him about the pictures of me playing with my first little girlfriend."

"Those were taken right here, weren't they?" She looked around the room. The carpet had changed, and the furniture was different, but it looked to her like the same place.

"Yeah, other than my years in the dorm, this is the only house I've ever lived in. Well, until I married you, of course." He sighed. "I guess I need to send these to my mom somehow." Of course, he'd have to find them first, and get them to give him an address to send things to.

"Do you know where your parents are now? Savannah said something about them traveling around the US in an RV."

Jake grinned. "They are. I haven't talked to them in a while. I don't think they even know we're married yet." He shrugged. "I should probably call them and find out what they want me to do with stuff before I sell the house."

"You're selling it?" The last she'd heard he hadn't been certain. She hoped he wasn't doing it just because he thought she wanted him to. She didn't care either way, but neither of them really had time to do any upkeep on it, and it would be tough from Manhattan.

"Yeah. I mean, there are a lot of memories here, but unless my parents want to move back in, there's no point in keeping it." He didn't really want to let it go, but he had no desire to keep it either.

"Yeah, you need to call them then. They might want to know you're married too. Unless you're keeping me your dirty little secret that is."

He laughed. "I could keep you hidden forever! Really though? The reason I haven't told them is Mom will want to meet you right away. I wanted you all to myself for a while first." No one needed their parents interfering during the first few weeks of their marriage.

"You wanted to finish your book first!" she protested. She knew him better than he thought she did.

"Well, that too," he said sheepishly. "I'll call." He leaned back on the couch, sticking one leg out, so he could dig his phone from his pocket. "I'm almost afraid."

Addie laughed, shaking her head. "I'll protect you." She looked back at the album while she unashamedly listened to his conversation.

"Hi, Mom. Where are you guys? Really? I had no idea. I'm at the house, packing things up. I got married last month and moved to Manhattan. Didn't see a reason to have two houses, so I was going to sell this one. No way! That sounds great. Yeah, her name is Addie. What does she look like? She has dark hair and brown eyes. To me she looks like an angel who fell from heaven. How did you know she's sitting here? Yeah. Okay, we'll see you then. Bye, Mom."

"What did she say?" Addie asked. It sounded like he'd made plans with them, but what were the chances they were in Montana?

Jake shook his head. "Would you believe they're driving through Billings right now? They were on their way home to surprise me."

She laughed. "My mom wants to know where I am all the time. She certainly knows what state I'm in and when I'm there. I can't believe how blasé your family is." Didn't they worry about each other?

"We're meeting them at the diner for lunch in thirty minutes," he told her, his eyes twinkling.

She jumped to her feet. "Thirty minutes? I've been packing boxes all morning. I'm covered in dust!" She put a hand to her heart to calm it. She couldn't meet her in-laws looking the way she did. "I'm going to shower. Be right back."

"Do you need someone to wash your back for you? 'Cuz, I would willingly sacrifice myself to do that for you."

She put her hand on his chest. "Down, big boy. I think I've got it!" She didn't mind the idea of showering with him, of course, but they didn't have time for what would inevitably follow.

"Are you sure? I don't want you to be embarrassed in front of Mom and Dad."

"I'm sure." She hurried into the bathroom and showered. Why hadn't she thought to bring a blow dryer? Oh yeah, because she hadn't thought she'd do anything but pack boxes.

Fifteen minutes later, she was back in the living room dressed in linen shorts and a tank top. She hated knowing she didn't look her best, but she hadn't even brought make-up with her. She was packing all weekend for goodness sake!

"You look beautiful," Jake told her, kissing her

cheek. "Don't be nervous." He truly thought she was the most beautiful woman he'd ever seen, whether she had make-up or not. She was a natural beauty.

"I'll do my best," she smoothed her shorts down. Why hadn't she brought longer shorts with her? She felt so conspicuous.

She could barely speak during the short drive to the diner. As they got out of the truck, Jake looked around. "I think we beat them. Let's go get a table."

As soon as they walked in, a woman about Jake's age in a waitress uniform hurried over. "I heard you got married, Jake! Introduce me to your bride."

Jake gave a half-smile. "Jennifer, this is my wife, Addie. Addie, this is Jennifer. She went to school with Scott and I." He said a quick prayer that Jennifer would keep her lips zipped for a bit. He knew it would take a lightning bolt through her forehead or spontaneous laryngitis for it to happen, but God could do *anything*.

Jennifer took Addie's hand. "It's so nice to finally meet you! You picked a winner. Let me tell you, if I'd known scrawny Jake was going to end up being a famous writer, I'd have gone to at least one of the dances he invited me to. He told us all he'd be a famous writer one day, but who believes the class nerd?"

"Table for four please, Jennifer." Jake refused to let her speak for another moment.

"Oh, did I say something wrong? I guess your wife didn't need to know all of that about you, huh? Sorry, Jake. I didn't mean to give away all your secrets." Jennifer led them to a booth in the corner. Addie slid in and Jake sat down beside her. "Coke and?" she looked at Addie.

"I'll just have water." Addie's hand went to Jake's under the table. As Jennifer walked away, she whispered. "Was she really pretty in high school? She must have been for you to overlook that personality." In her mind she called her a choice name.

Jake shrugged, embarrassed by what Jennifer had said.

Addie's eyes grew wide. "She was your Boring Bob the Boob, wasn't she?" She knew he was embarrassed, and she wanted to get his mind off the other woman. Jennifer wasn't worth him feeling bad over.

He laughed at the imagery. "Well, kind of. Except I thought she was the most beautiful girl ever, and she didn't know I existed. Until she decided she was in love with Scott, and then she was nice to me so I could help her get him to ask her to a dance. He took her out once and told her she was too stuck up."

Addie grinned. "What did you think of that?"

"Honestly? It was the only fight Scott and I had all through high school, and we didn't speak for weeks. I didn't think he should treat her that way, because in my mind she was a princess. When I told her that, she laughed. Said she couldn't be seen with me without Scott." He shrugged. "I learned a lot from her." He learned a lot about not trusting women. He learned not to believe anything anyone said to him once he made serious money as well.

"Sounds like it wasn't a fun lesson."

"Nope. But after I'd published my third book, and it hit the *New York Times Best Sellers List?* Well that's when she decided that we needed to give our relationship a chance." He made a face. "She'd already been married and divorced by then."

"Oh lovely. Yeah, I don't think I want to get to know her at all." She looked up and saw a couple standing over the table. "Are those your parents?"

Jake stood up and was swallowed up in a bear hug by a man who must have been close to six and a half feet tall. When he pulled away he was embraced by a woman who was barely five feet and almost as wide as she was tall. Addie couldn't help but be struck by the couple, and how genuinely odd they looked together.

Addie didn't know if she should stand or remain seated, so she stayed where she was until invited to do otherwise. She was pleased to see that his parents looked like down to earth people. She wanted nothing more than to get along with them, because she knew they were important to Jake. And anyone who was important to Jake automatically became important to her.

His mother slid into the booth across from her and offered her hand across the table. "I'm Beverly."

Addie smiled. "I'm Addie. It's really nice to meet you." She'd have added she'd heard a lot about her if it had been true. The truth was, Jake hadn't told her much about his parents at all. She hoped they would be easy to get to know.

"It's nice to meet you too! How did you and Jake meet? Were you at Scott's wedding when he married that stranger last summer?" Beverly didn't seem to think there was anything wrong with Scott marrying a stranger, but still, Addie was unsure how to respond to the pointed question.

"No, we...um," Addie couldn't finish her sentence. How did you tell a woman that you met her son at the altar when you married him?

Thankfully Jake took the seat beside her and answered for her. "We were set up by the same matchmaker who set up Scott and Savannah. We met at the altar, just like they did." He knew his mother would be surprised, but she knew his issues with trusting women, so maybe she'd understand.

Beverly's eyes grew wide. "Really? I'll bet that was strange. Probably took you a few days to work up to sex, right?" She looked back and forth between Jake and Addie like she expected one of them to give her information about their wedding night.

Addie blushed, looking at Jake for help. She couldn't talk to his mother about having sex with him! "I..." What was she supposed to say to that? She was almost ready to lie to the woman and tell her they hadn't worked up to it yet, but they were getting there!

Jake's father sat down. "Don't mind her. She has absolutely no filter. If a thought pops into her head, it comes out her mouth." He reached across the table, his hand as big as a dinner plate. "I'm Tom."

She shook his hand, working hard not to look at Beverly. She couldn't believe the woman was even asking about her sex life. She truly had no boundaries. "It's nice to meet you."

"And you." Tom picked up the menu from the table in front of him. "Are the bison burgers still good?"

Jake nodded, and Addie noticed that his face was

red too. He must feel the same way she did about talking about their sex lives with his mother. And who could blame him? "Yeah, still awesome. That's what I would get," Jake answered.

Beverly studied the menu and finally closed it. "I'm getting the meat loaf. It's always been my favorite thing on their menu."

Addie decided to try again with his mother, so she leaned forward and whispered, "I promise not to tell Scott you ate beef."

Beverly let out a loud laugh. "Thank you for that. I don't need to have that boy mad at me." She looked at Jake. "Do you think Scott would mind if we dry docked the RV at his place for the next few days? We were planning on staying at the house, but that's probably not a good idea with the two of you staying there. You're still newlyweds, and we wouldn't want to disturb—"

Tom shook his head, putting his hand over his wife's mouth. "I swear she's more outspoken every year."

Addie felt a bubble of laughter coming up. Both of the men at the table were as embarrassed as she was over the older woman's conversation. Had she been about to say that she wouldn't want to disturb their sex lives? Really?

Jennifer came back then, dropping off her drink and Jake's. "Oh, it's good to see you, Mr. and Mrs. Roberts! I didn't realize you were back in town!"

Beverly looked at Jennifer with a gleam in her eye. "Well, look at that. My little boy's high school crush serving us in a restaurant. He's a best-selling author who pulls in millions, and you're working for waitress minimum. Isn't life strange that way? The way it just turns things around and pokes you right in the eye?"

Addie noticed no one tried to stop Beverly that time, and she was glad. She wasn't a vengeful person, but the way Jennifer had talked to them when they first came in, made her pleased she was getting some of her own back.

Jennifer blinked twice, and smiled her fake smile. "It is strange how life turns things around when you least expect it. Can I get you something to drink?" She was obviously in retreat mode now, and just needed to get them their food.

"We'll both have Cokes," Tom said, and Addie silently cheered him. He didn't apologize for his wife, but neither did he add to what she said.

Jake acted as if nothing had happened, but Addie could see the humor in his eyes. "I think Scott would welcome you with open arms. He loves you both." He held up his phone. "Want me to call him?"

Tom nodded. "Would you? That would smooth our way in. Not that we need it with a boy who was like a second son to us, but it would be nice."

"Excuse me. I'll call from outside." Jake looked at Addie before standing. "Would you order for me? Bison burger medium rare."

Addie wrinkled her nose at the way he wanted it cooked, but she nodded anyway. Then she realized she was sitting there alone with his parents. What could she say to them? "How long will you be in Montana?" she asked.

Tom shrugged. "We have no definite plans. Maybe a week, maybe a month. You just never know."

Beverly looked at her. "How long will the two of you be in town?"

"Just through Wednesday. We want to get everything packed up, and then find an apartment. I need to be back at work on Monday." Would they have a problem with her working? With as much as Jake made, she certainly didn't need to. Her mother would surely point that out to her again the next time they were alone.

"Where are you living now?" Beverly asked, raising an eyebrow.

"We're in a really small apartment in Manhattan

that I subleased for two months. Jake wants something bigger, so we're finding something else." Addie shrugged. "I'm sure we'll find something that suits him better. He hates having to work in the living room, and I really don't blame him. I make noise as I cook, clean, and do my work. I'm sure it'll be nice for him to be off in his own space."

"What do you do?" Tom asked her, obviously curious and not just making idle conversation.

"I own a craft store where we teach classes on the different crafts. We have an in-store child care where children can be dropped off for up to two hours while Mom shops or takes a class. We also teach mommy and me classes a couple of times a week." Addie's pride in the store came through in her voice.

Beverly smiled. "That sounds really nice. I remember trying to shop when Jake was little and it was a nightmare. I'd like to see your store someday."

"I'd love to show it to you." Addie hadn't expected to get along with her mother-in-law, just because she'd heard so many stories about how evil they were. She was pleasantly surprised that hers wasn't bad at all. A little more out-spoken than she'd like, but she seemed to be a kind woman.

Jake came back then, sliding back into the booth and putting his arm across the back of it, over Addie's shoulders. "Scott said you're welcome to stay just as long as you'd like."

"Oh, good! I can't wait to see Scott. Did Savannah have the baby?" Beverly looked at Jake, waiting for the news on her friend's grandchild.

"Yes, she had a boy, and they named him Kaeden. He looks just like Scott did." Jake nodded at Addie. "She found the old photo albums and was looking through them this morning. We were making fun of Scott's girlish looks."

Beverly smiled. "He was such a cute baby with those blond curls!" She turned her gaze to Addie. "When can we expect grandbabies?"

Addie bit her lip, almost afraid to answer. "We decided that we'd wait to start trying 'til we've been married a year. I'm only twenty-five, so we have plenty of time." She held her breath, waiting for her mother-in-law's reaction. Would she be angry that they were waiting? Or would she accept that it was their decision?

"And after you have them? Will you keep your store?"

"Yes, I will. I think we'll probably hire a nanny." She shrugged. "Hopefully a live-in, because we all know how much help Jake would be with a newborn."

Beverly seemed to think about her new daughter-in-law's answer for a moment, before a slow smile spread across her face. "I approve. I don't think a woman should have to give up something she loves to stay home with her children."

Addie was surprised Beverly had such a different view than her own mother. "I agree. Did you work outside the home when Jake was small?"

Beverly shook her head. "I didn't. I wanted to, but there was so much pressure saying that I needed to stay home with Jake for him to be a well-rounded individual. So I stayed home. I wanted to work, and I enjoyed working, but instead I did the stay at home mom thing, and we made financial sacrifices." She looked at Jake. "Do you think things would have been different if I'd worked?"

Jake shook his head. "No, because you would have made it clear you loved me no matter what. That's all that really mattered." His mother had loved him more than he'd realized at the time. They'd made sacrifice after sacrifice for him. He had nothing but respect for both of his parents.

"I'm glad you can see that!" Beverly said. "I wish my mother could have."

"Did Grandma try to force you to stay home with me?" Jake had never imagined she'd been pressured to do something she didn't want to do because of him. It bothered him to think about it.

"Yes, she used every kind of guilt imaginable. I don't know why people always think they know better than the child's parents. Before you were born, we had it worked out that Lisa, Scott's mom, would stay home with both of you, and I would go back to work as a real estate agent. My mother threw such a fit that I ended up bending to her will though."

"I didn't know that," Jake said.

Beverly shrugged. "It was a long time ago, and you were always very close to your grandmother. I wasn't about to tell you what she said."

"Well, I'm going to do what we think I should do," Addie said. "We may change our minds when the time comes, but for now, I'm going to keep working."

"I think you should!"

Addie looked at Jake, trying to convey to him how pleased she was that his mother was willing to let her make her own decisions about what they'd do when they had children.

"I'm so glad you happened to be in Montana while we were here," Addie told Beverly. "So happy that I got to meet you."

"Are we what you expected?" Beverly asked.

"Not at all. You're so much better."

Chapter Nine

For the next three days, Addie worked alongside Beverly to get the house packed, while Jake and Tom worked on the garage. Slowly but surely the work was done. When they'd packed the last box and assigned it to storage or to be shipped to New York, Addie looked around at the barren house. "Are you sure you're ready for this?" she asked Beverly.

"I think so. We talked about selling when we started on our RVing adventures, but we wanted Jake to have the continuity. And honestly? At this point in our travels, we could use the money from the sale."

"Oh, that never occurred to me. How do you fund your travels?" Addie forgot that Jake and his family hadn't always had money. Of course, the house he'd grown up in should have told her that. It was in good shape, but it was tiny.

Beverly smiled. "I was very frugal as a housewife. I clipped every coupon, and I budgeted every dime. I socked money away in the stock market every month. We've been living on the dividends from those all these years. We're about to have to touch the principle, and I'd rather not do that."

"I see. The sales from the house would go far to keep that from happening." Addie had no idea what it would cost to live on the road the way her in-laws did, but she knew they did it as frugally as they could.

"Yes, they would. Eventually we'll have to settle down like normal old people, but I don't think it's going to happen here in Montana. When we settle it's going to be closer to wherever our grandbabies will be. Upstate New York is beautiful and only a few hours from you."

Addie smiled, reaching out to hug her mother-in-law. "I wasn't sure how I was going to feel about you at first. Now I know that I'm thrilled to have you in my life." Who would have thought a dreaded mother-in-law could be so sweet and kind?

"Why weren't you sure how you were going to feel about me?"

"Well, within a few minutes of meeting, you were asking me about sex with your son. That made me a little uncomfortable." Addie had a hard time even mentioning that sex existed to her mother-in-law, let alone giving details.

Beverly smiled. "I guess I can see how it would. You're still not going to tell me how sex with him is, are you?"

"No, I never am. Thank you ever so much for respecting that." Addie's eyes twinkled as she shut down the conversation once again.

Beverly sighed. "Honestly? If you'd told me, I'd have had a problem with you. Sometimes being outrageous is just a test to see what people are made of. Sometimes it's revenge for the way people have treated my family. But I promise, there's always a reason for it."

Addie laughed. "Does Jake know that?" She loved knowing that the older woman wasn't just clueless about social niceties. She did it all on purpose, and that made it even better in her eyes.

"Of course not. He thinks I'm eccentric. That's all right too. Sometimes it just doesn't matter." Beverly smiled. "What time is your flight tomorrow?"

"Nine in the morning. It'll be early evening before we get home. We have an appointment with a realtor for Thursday morning. I think Jake is going to feel a lot more settled once we find our new place." Addie was looking forward to finding something bigger as well. It would be nice to have room to invite people over. It wasn't like Jake would even notice!

"Oh he will. My boy is very picky about where he writes." Beverly shook her head. "I'm surprised he was able to finish a book in the living room. When we lived here, he wrote in his bedroom with the door locked, and I had to sneak into his room the next day while he was at school to read what he'd written. He should have just let me read it!"

"Yeah, he hates for anyone to read it until the editor has gone through it. Was he always that way?" Addie had never known a professional writer before, so she had no idea if how he acted was normal or just a little bit on the crazy side.

"Yes, he was. It made me crazy."

Addie realized she needed to tell Jake how she'd discovered he was really Roger Holiday. She'd blamed him so much for betraying her trust, but hadn't she done the same thing by reading his book without his permission? She needed to talk to him about it. "I'm a big fan of his books, so it makes me crazy as well," she said absently. "I'd love to get to read every chapter as soon as he finished writing it, but he's made it very clear that's never going to happen."

"Well, now that we're finally finished here, we should go spend the day with Savannah. Maybe we could watch Kaeden while Scott and Savannah have a date night tonight. How would you feel about that?"

Addie nodded. "I think that's a great idea if they want to do it. Let's stop at the grocery store so we can feed ourselves without raiding their kitchen. It'll be fun to cook together." Much to her surprise, she genuinely enjoyed spending time with her mother-in-law. Most people she knew would have said it just wasn't possible.

"In Savannah's big kitchen it will be. It wouldn't in the small one here. This one is a one butt kitchen. Two people would never fit!"

Addie grinned. She loved the quirky little things her mother-in-law said. "Let me call Savannah and see if she wants company. If she does, then we'll head over."

Five minutes later, they had their plan. They would go to the grocery store, and then they would cook dinner for themselves at Savannah's. Savannah would feed the baby, and then she and Scott would go out to dinner. They would do their best to make it back before Kaeden's next feeding.

The men were sitting on the front steps when they walked outside. "All done?" Addie asked, nudging Jake with her foot.

"Yup. We finished about fifteen minutes ago. Taking a break, and then we're going to come in and help with the rest of the packing."

"We're finished too," Addie said. "I just talked to Savannah, and we want to go out there and spend the day with them. Your mom and I are going to watch the baby tonight while Savannah and Scott have some time alone together." She knew it would be fun to share the baby with the older woman. Hopefully someday they'd be sharing her and Jake's baby.

Jake groaned good-naturedly. "Do you have to?"

"Yep. We're cooking dinner too, so we have to stop for groceries on the way." She nudged him with her foot again, trying to get him to move faster. Men said women were slow to do things, but he was the one sitting on the steps like a lump.

"Fine. We'll go grocery shopping and then head out to the ranch." Jake looked at his father. "Do we always have to just do what they want us to do?"

"If we want to have peaceful marriages we do. I love you, dear. Yes, dear." Tom winked at Beverly over his shoulder.

*****

An hour later they converged on the ranch in two vehicles. Jake and Tom carried in the groceries while the women went in to talk to Savannah. "Thank you so much for watching the baby," Savannah said with a smile. "We haven't had a night out alone since we were in Manhattan for your wedding."

"Who watched him them? Dr. Lachele?" Addie asked. She couldn't imagine how hard it would be to be with a baby twenty-four hours a day like Savannah was. She just didn't think she was cut out for it.

"No, my mom and her new husband watched him." Savannah smiled. "I think if I hadn't married Scott, my mom would still be spending all her time trying to meddle in my life. I'm glad I took the leap."

"I'm glad I did too," Addie told her. "Even though I ended up with a crazy writer like Jake." Not that she would change a single thing about her new husband.

Beverly smiled. "You and Jake are good for each other."

"We are." Addie thought about what she needed to talk to him about and wondered how angry he would be. She realized she'd betrayed his trust as much as he'd betrayed hers. They needed to talk once they were home. She didn't want to leave a bad feeling in anyone's mind about the Montana trip. "Where's Scott?"

Savannah shrugged. "I think he's showering. He came in early today so he could be ready when you got here. He wants to make the most of our night out."

"Good! He was all for it then?"

Savannah laughed. "He asked if we could take a week."

Addie grinned. "Did you tell him the baby would starve? And that I need to go back to work on Monday?"

"I did. He said that was sad, because we really need a baby-free week. Not just a couple of hours." Savannah grinned. "He'd do better if we could just find a good sitter around here."

"Do you expect to find one?" Addie asked. She didn't know much about the area.

"Not really. I don't really want a high school girl watching him, and everyone else is too busy. It's fine, though. We get occasional help, and that's good enough. Now if we had more children? We might just need to get a nanny."

Scott walked into the room just then. "Why would we get a nanny? You're a great mom. Besides, why have kids if you're just going to have someone else raise them?"

Addie felt like she was listening to her mother all over again, but this time she had the right to stand up to him. She couldn't disrespect her mother by arguing. "Because it's all right to have a career and children as well. Because it doesn't make you any less of a parent if you don't spend twenty-four hours a day with your child. Are you less of a father because you aren't with Kaeden all day?" She knew her voice was sharper than it needed to be, but Scott was one of those people who pushed her buttons.

"Well, no, but I'm the man. It's my job to support my family. It's Savannah's job to stay home with Kaeden and make sure we're fed and the house is always clean." Scott spoke slowly as if he were trying to explain the universe to a small child.

Addie closed her eyes and counted to ten before she walked over to Scott and stood toe to toe with the big man. "I'm so sorry you're still living in the early twentieth century, Scott. I don't know how women's liberation and the entrance of women into the workplace has escaped you, but it obviously has. You are without a doubt, the most Neanderthal-like man I've ever encountered. If I didn't like your wife so much, I'd...I'd...Well, I'd do something!" She walked over to Jake. "You need to control your friend. He's ridiculous."

Jake nodded. "He is sometimes. Aren't you glad I don't think like him?" As much as he loved his wife, he couldn't imagine being with her twenty-four hours per day every day. Wait...love? Where had that thought come from? He paled. He couldn't love her. They'd only known one another a month!

"Very glad. I'd have killed you by now if I had

to live with that attitude. I'm every bit as capable as any man, penis or no penis!"

Jake folded her into his arms, hugging her close and kissing her forehead. "Yes, you are." He leaned forward and put his lips against her ear, whispering, "Don't say penis in front of my mom. You'll get her started all over again!"

Beverly looked back and forth between her new daughter-in-law and Scott. "Speaking of penises, I forgot to show you the album I have of naked pictures of Jake. He was still running around naked all the time at eleven. We could *not* get him to leave his clothes on around the house or in the backyard, so I have some good ones!"

Addie started to laugh, still in Jake's arms, loving the blush on his face. "You know what, Beverly?"

"No..."

"If I had six mother-in-laws, you'd still be my favorite!" Addie couldn't believe how easily she'd gotten over her anger by laughing. Her mother in law definitely knew how to handle her after only a few days.

Beverly grinned. "Well, of course, I would. Who could compare with all this?" She swept her hands down over her plump form.

Addie leaned forward and whispered, "I love

your mother!"

Jake laughed. "I get that a lot."

*****

Addie waited until they got home before confessing what she'd done to Jake. Her hands were shaking, and she could barely get the words out, but he needed to know.

They sat together on the couch, and she turned to him. "I need to tell you something. I should have told you long ago, but I didn't think about how important it was until I was talking to your mother yesterday."

Jake's heart started to beat faster. He needed to tell her something too. She needed to know he loved her. "I need to say something to you too. I'll let you go first, though." He took both her hands in his, giving her his full attention. *Please God, let her say she loves me first. I'm not sure I can put myself out there unless I know the feelings are returned.*

Addie took a deep breath. "Our first Friday back in Manhattan? When I was finding a restaurant for us to eat at? I thought I'd use your computer rather than trying to see what I needed to see on my tiny phone screen or pulling out my laptop. When I sat down, your document was up from where you'd been writing, and I read through over a page before I stopped myself. That's how I knew you were Roger Holiday. I'm so sorry!"

Jake shook his head for a moment as if to clear his mind. "You mean, you did something I'd asked you not to do, and then you got mad at me and said you couldn't trust me? So you not only betrayed *my* trust, you made a big deal at the same time about me betraying yours?" He wasn't angry, but he was hurt. How could she accuse him when she'd done something wrong as well?

"It didn't even occur to me I'd done something that would upset you until I talked to your mother yesterday." A lone tear rolled down her cheek. "We were talking about how private you are about what you're writing, and it occurred to me that I was as bad as she was."

"As bad as she was? What do you mean by that?"

"When she would sneak into your room and read what you wrote when you left for school."

"She wouldn't do that. My mother has more respect for me than that." Why would she try to make him angry with his mother? She'd done nothing wrong!

Addie closed her eyes. She'd just betrayed his mother as well. What was wrong with her? She said nothing else about what his mother had done, and instead focused on herself. "Well, while we were talking about how you felt about people who read what you are working on, I realized that I'd done something that you would abhor. I needed to tell you I'd done it. Will you forgive me?"

Jake shook his head. "I don't know that I can! Especially not with you trying to drag my mother into it! What is *wrong* with you?" He hadn't been angry until she'd started making accusations about his mother!

Addie looked at him, hating herself. "I'm sorry. I can't say much more than that."

"I'm going to go for a walk. I'll be back later." Jake walked out the door and left without another word. She had no idea where he was going or when he'd be back.

She dried her tears and reached for her phone. She had to get help. She quickly touched her speed dial for the only person she could think of who might be able to give her some insight about what to do. "Dr. Lachele?"

"Addie? Is that you? Why are you crying?"

"I need some advice. I've messed up really

badly." Addie sniffled again, reaching for a Kleenex to dry her eyes.

"Meet me at the restaurant where we had lunch with Danielle. Can you be there in thirty minutes?"

Addie thought for a moment about where the restaurant was. "Yes. It's only a fifteen minute walk from here. I'll see you there." She ended the call and went into the bathroom, using a cold wash cloth to try to help her eyes. They were bloodshot and her cheeks were red from crying.

She carefully locked the door behind her and headed toward the restaurant, arriving there a few minutes early. She looked around, but couldn't see the familiar purple hair, so she got a table for two.

She was led to a small table in one corner, and she sat down, looking at her phone and not making eye contact with anyone. She always felt funny sitting alone in a restaurant, almost like people were looking at her as if she couldn't find a friend.

She didn't have to wait long before the hostess brought Dr. Lachele, and the older woman took the seat across from her, automatically squeezing her hand. "Let's order, and then you can tell me everything that's happened."

Addie nodded, studying the menu. She didn't feel like soup, and that was her usual there, so she needed to find something different. She finally settled on a club sandwich and set the menu aside.

Dr. Lachele put hers down too. "What happened? I'm surprised this is the first I've heard from you really, but I expected anger, not tears. Tell me everything!"

Addie explained about how odd Jake was while writing. She talked about his long hours, his inability to even acknowledge someone was there, and his deception about who he really was.

"So you're angry about all that? And that's why you're crying?"

Addie shook her head. "No! He's mad at me for betraying him!" Addie never cried when she was angry. She was more likely to start yelling with anger.

Dr. Lachele blinked. "Okay, you left something out. Help me understand. How did you betray him?" She clearly didn't understand the problem.

"Jake has this thing about never let anyone read what he's working on. The first person to see it is always his editor, and if someone tries to read it, he gets really angry. Well, I knew that, but I was in a hurry to find a good restaurant near our apartment one evening, oh it was three or four weeks ago now. Anyway, I sat down at his computer to use the internet, and I just started reading. I didn't mean to, but his document was up. Well, that's how I found out he was Roger Holiday. I confronted him about his lies, and his lack of trust." Addie looked down at her hands. "I may have even called him a lying pig. It's unclear now. Anyway, I didn't tell him how I knew, not thinking that was important."

"I can see how you'd have deliberately forgotten telling him that," Dr. Lachele said encouragingly. "When did you realize your mistake?"

"Not until yesterday! I was talking to his mom, and she told me how she used to sneak in his room when he left the house so she could read whatever he was working on. She said it was the only way she could keep up with his work. And it occurred to me that I'd done something just as bad. I hadn't meant to, but I had. So I decided that as soon as we got home, I'd tell him."

"Where were you?" Dr. Lachele asked, obviously getting distracted.

"Montana, packing up his parents' house, and they showed up. I love them!" Addie had to make it clear just how much she liked her new in-laws.

"I knew you would! They're such lovely people!" Lachele shook her head, trying to force her mind back on track. "So did you tell him?"

Addie nodded. "He's really mad. He left, said he was going for a walk." She sighed. "I've really messed up."

The waitress came by then to take their orders. As soon as she was gone, Addie looked back at Dr. Lachele. "What do I do now?" She felt bereft. They'd been doing so well, and now she'd just blown it.

"I can't tell you what to do. You know that. Do you think he should be mad at you?"

"Definitely. And I told him about his mother sneaking into his room, and he didn't even know she'd done that. So now I feel like I've betrayed her as well!" Addie wondered if she should call his mother. She probably needed to know that she'd told him about her, assuming he already knew.

"Okay, so you got angry with him when you felt he betrayed you weeks ago. How long did you stay angry with him?"

Addie thought about it. "Forty-eight hours? Not long. I feel too much for him to stay angry long." She really wasn't certain what that had to do with anything, but Dr. Lachele obviously knew what she was doing with counseling.

"Have you told him?"

"Told him...?" Addie asked.

"Have you told him you love him? I know you've said you're sorry. You're the type of person who would say that first, but if you really put your feelings and emotions out there, it might help you." Dr. Lachele shrugged. "It's probably just going to be a matter of time. He gave you forty-eight hours. Can you do the same for him?"

Addie nodded slowly. "I can. The difference is, during his forty-eight hours, he was busy working and barely paid any attention to me. During my forty-eight hours, we're apartment hunting. We'll be around each other a lot more while he's mad." She wasn't sure how she'd handle it if he acted angry and cold the whole time.

"Well, in my professional opinion, you should stop and buy yourself something really sexy on your way home. As soon as you get home, change into it, and crawl into his lap. He's a man; nature will take its course."

"How will that make him less mad at me?" Addie asked, confused.

"It might not! But it will help break the tension, and you'll be able to be around each other easier. If he's still mad, which he really probably will be, just wait him out. But while you're doing the horizontal mambo? Tell him you love him. It'll mean the world to him."

"Do you really think that will work? Won't he think I'm just messing with his emotions?" She didn't want him angry with her, but she needed to make sure she wasn't only making things worse.

Dr. Lachele shook her head. "Men don't think that way. He'll just be glad that he's getting some."

Addie chuckled softly. "You have an interesting way of looking at things for a purple haired lady with a PhD in psychology."

"What can I say? I'm unique!"

*****

Jake wandered through the streets of Manhattan, angry enough to kick someone. How dare she read his manuscript without his permission, and worse? How dare she accuse his mother of reading his writing whenever he left the house? He knew his mother would never do that!

Pulling his phone from his pocket, he hit the speed dial for his mother's cell phone. "Hi, Mom."

"You sound down. What's wrong with you?"

"Can I ask you something? I need an honest answer. Well, a couple of somethings." Jake didn't want to have this conversation, but maybe his mother could help him figure a couple of things out.

"What's that? You know I'll tell you the truth. Being blunt is my signature action."

"Well, what did you think of Addie? Did you like her?"

Beverly laughed. "I loved her. She was made for you. Why would you even ask me that? Couldn't you see how much I liked her?"

Jake smiled. "Yeah, I could. Now, for the hard question. Have you ever read one of my stories before it was finished?"

There was a pause on the other end of the phone, and finally she answered him. "Every single time you wrote one. As soon as you left for school, I was in your room, reading every word you'd written. How could I not? You're a wonderful writer, and I love you. Naturally I want to read what you've written."

Jake shook his head. Leave it to his mother to act as if doing something he specifically asked her not to do was a compliment. "Why didn't you ever tell me you did it?"

"Because I knew you'd get mad at me, of course. Would you have told you?"

Jake sighed. "Probably not. Okay, thanks. Have

a good time in Montana."

"I plan on it. And Jakey?"

He cringed at the use of his childhood nickname. "Yeah, Mom?"

"Forgive her. Whatever she did? Love is worth it."

The phone was dead in his hand. He looked at it for a minute, before turning around and walking back toward the apartment. His crazy mother was right. Love was worth anything.

He moved through the tall buildings all lit up against the night. He loved his wife, and love was worth it. He needed to tell her he loved her.

By the time their building was in sight, he was jogging. He wanted to tell her quickly. He couldn't let her suffer by thinking he was mad at her. He knew how hard it was. Why, it had taken him longer to write the end of his book than it should have, because he was so worried about her. He wouldn't make her worry a minute longer than necessary.

He took the stairs two at a time, not wanting to have to wait for the elevator. Finally, he stood on the fifth floor outside their door. He reached for the door knob. Locked. What?

He knocked once and waited for her. When there

was no response, he pounded. "Addie! Let me in!"

Chapter Ten

Addie got out of the elevator, the bag with her new lingerie in it tucked into her purse. She didn't want him to know she'd purchased it until she was wearing it for him. As she walked down the hall toward the apartment, she heard pounding. She hadn't noticed any of the neighbors being loud, so she was surprised. Who could be causing such a commotion?

She turned the corner into their hallway, and there was Jake, standing in the hall, pounding on their door. Her eyes widened. She'd never gotten around to giving him a key!

She hurried down the hall. "Jake, I'm here. I meant to be back before you. I'm so sorry!"

He turned and looked her up and down, as if he expected something to be wrong with her. "Where were you?"

"I was upset, so I went to meet a friend. I needed to talk."

He sighed, relieved. "I don't have a key." He knew it was obvious, but he felt like an idiot standing there in the hall having just pounded on their door for her to let him in.

She grinned. "I see that. I told you I had one for you, but we never got around to it." She opened the door and walked in. "We should talk. Let me get your key first though, so I don't forget again. Wait here." She went into the bedroom and closed the door behind her. She knew he must be wondering what she was doing as she quickly changed into the negligee.

She grabbed the key from her jewelry box and took a deep breath, before going back into the living room to give him the key. And shock him. She'd do that too.

She hadn't worn anything sexy for him since their honeymoon. Half the time he hadn't seemed to know she was there, so why bother? She walked over to where he sat on the couch, and stood in front of him, holding the key out for him. "Now, don't leave without it, unless we're together."

Jake's eyes took in her change of clothing. "What's this about?"

Addie shrugged. "I thought I'd get something new while I was out. Do you like it?" She spun in a slow circle for him so he could see her entire outfit.

He swallowed hard, his Adam's apple bobbing.

"I love it." The short, satiny nightgown was turquoise with spaghetti straps. "We need to talk before I show you just how much I love it." He grabbed her hand and pulled her down into his lap, holding her close.

"Can I go first?" she asked.

He nodded. "I believe ladies should always go first. In everything." He kissed the side of her neck while he waited for her to speak.

She was surprised he was so calm now when he'd been eaten up with anger just a couple of hours before. "I want to say one more time that I'm sorry. I didn't sit down to read what you wrote. It just kind of happened."

"I can understand that. Will you try not to do it again?"

She nodded. "I will. I love you too much to do anything that will upset you." It seemed that he'd already forgiven her, and she was thankful for that. She was glad he wasn't as stubborn as her, staying angry for hours instead of days.

His eyes widened. "What did you just say? Did you say you love me?" They were the words he'd been waiting for, but now that he thought he'd heard them, he had to verify.

"Yes. Is that a bad thing?"

He shook his head. "That's what I wanted to say to you." He pulled her head down for a tender kiss, no tongue and no hands grabbing her. Just lips meeting sweetly. "I love you, Addie. More than I could ever express."

She turned fully onto his lap to face him, one knee going to either side of his thighs so she could look into his eyes. "You're not mad at me anymore?"

He shook his head. "I talked to my mom. She admitted that she used to read whatever I wrote as soon as I left the house. I never knew. Why would she do that?"

Addie smiled. "Because she loved you and thought you were very talented."

"That's what she said." He stroked her cheek with one finger. It was hard to believe she loved him. She was so beautiful. He'd never once had to doubt her feelings for him. He knew he shouldn't be glad about deceiving her at the beginning of their marriage, but he was. He should have told her sooner, yes, but he was glad he hadn't told her immediately. He didn't think he'd ever have been able to trust her otherwise. "Do you know what else she said?" he asked.

"What?"

"She said that you were perfect for me, and I

needed to fight for you, no matter what you did wrong. Because love's worth fighting for." He looked deeply into her eyes. "I think it is."

"Thank you for being so kind about it. Once I realized just what I'd done, I told you as soon as I felt like I could."

"I know you did. You did everything just right. I'm sorry I stormed off."

"Sorry you stormed off, because it upset me? Or sorry you stormed off because you didn't have a key and got locked out?"

Jake laughed. "Maybe a bit of both? Regardless, I *am* sorry. Thank you for not getting angry with me." He pulled her down for another kiss, appreciating her outfit. "Who did you go talk to anyway?" he asked.

"Dr. Lachele," she said, slightly embarrassed. "I was sure I'd ruined our relationship forever."

"Did she help you?"

She nodded. "Yeah, she did." She hoped he didn't ask what kind of advice Dr. Lachele gave, because that would embarrass her.

"I'm glad." He kissed her again, thrilled they were no longer fighting. "Wanna go hang out in the bedroom and 'talk' in there?"

"Sure. I love to talk to you." She got to her feet and took his hand, leading him toward the bedroom. "Does this mean that you'll pay more attention to me while you're writing a book?"

"Probably not. I mean, I can say I'll try, but I'd probably be lying." He winked at her when she glared at him.

"Can't blame a girl for hoping!"

"No, you can't!"

*****

She was exhausted by early afternoon the next day. They'd looked at fifteen apartments, and none were good enough. They were either too small, too bright, not enough bedrooms, the bedrooms were too small or her personal favorite, there were too many windows.

"How can you complain about windows? You need light to write by, don't you?"

"That's why Thomas Edison invented the light bulb."

She sighed. "We've only got one more apartment on our list. I would like to have this nailed down today, so we're ready to move on your next days off."

"I would too!" He sighed. "Well, someone is supposed to be meeting us here in just a few minutes to show us this last place. It's a sublease, but from what I understand we could have it indefinitely."

"Are we early?" Addie asked, looking around.

"No, but the guy said he might be late. He said he couldn't leave early, because the paper doesn't sell itself. I don't know what that means, and honestly? I don't want to."

"Paper? That's weird."

A man hurried around the corner. "Mr. and Mrs. Roberts? I'm Bob Archer."

Addie watched the man's face, wondering if he'd recognize her. Of course, he hadn't ever looked at her above her neck, so there wasn't much chance of that happening.

He unlocked the apartment. "Go in and look around. It was my grandfather's place, but he's in a nursing home now. We can't afford to keep paying rent this steep on it, so my brother and I are trying to sublease." He waved a hand toward the apartment, and they wandered in looking around.

It was a three bedroom two bath apartment with a balcony that overlooked Central Park. Addie fell in love immediately. It was exactly the kind of place she'd always dreamed of living. She held her breath as she waited for Jake to start listing all the reasons it wasn't good enough.

She trailed behind him as he opened every closet, and looked at every square inch of the walls. "I want it," he told her.

She almost squealed with delight, grabbing him in a bear hug. "Me too! I love this place!"

"Let's go see how much. Don't act excited now. We're likely to get a better rate if you act like you don't care much."

Addie nodded, knowing they'd really get a good rate if she lifted her shirt and showed her boobs, but she didn't tell her husband that.

Bob was leaning on the counter in the kitchen, doing something with his phone. "Probably looking at porn," she mumbled under her breath.

Jake gave her a warning look before asking, "How much?"

Bob named a figure that seemed much too high to Addie. He was playing them, which didn't surprise her at all.

By the time they left, Jake had talked Bob down to seventy-five percent of his initial price, and they had a moving date that fit their schedule well. As they stepped out into the sunshine, Addie sighed. "I can't believe we're renting from Boring Bob the Boob. I hope we don't have to see him much."

"Do you call all men named Bob that?" Jake asked in surprise.

Addie shook her head. "Nope. Just him."

"He didn't seem to recognize you," Jake said in confusion.

"I think he only looked at my face once, for about thirty seconds. The rest of the time he was staring at my chest. Why would he remember me?"

Jake shook his head with a sigh. "I wish I'd known. I'd never have agreed to rent from Boring Bob the Boob."

"Why not? If you think about it, I'd never have talked to Lachele if it hadn't been for Bob. He's the one who brought us together. We wouldn't have married without him."

Jake laughed. "Tonight when we eat, we're going to toast Boring Bob the Boob. If Lachele ever needs an assistant matchmaker, she should call on him. He'd drive every single woman in New York to seek out her business."

"I'll suggest it to her the next time we talk. She'd

probably go for it! Her purple hair indicates a deviant personality for sure."

"Definitely...I'll call her!"

Epilogue

One year later...

"Did you call your parents?" Addie asked Jake.

"I did. Mom is ecstatic. They're looking for a house in Upstate New York, so they can be close to us." Jake smiled. He really liked the idea of his parents playing a bigger role in their lives. "Did you call yours?"

She nodded. "Dad's thrilled. Mom thinks I should sell the store or find someone who can run it for me, so I don't have to leave the house."

"Don't take it hard. We knew she'd react that way."

Addie sighed. "We did know that." She patted her still-flat belly. "So we still need to tell Dr. Lachele, and I think she just may be more excited than the other two put together."

Jake grinned. "Oh, she will be. She's happy with her other Matchrimony Munchkins, but I think this is her first set of twin munchkins. I wonder what she'll call them. Multiple Munchkins?"

Addie giggled. "There's no telling. We need to call her though. Making two baby gifts will take twice as long! I'll call Scott and Savannah after Dr. Lachele. Our purple haired matchmaker deserves to know first."

"You do the honors. I just got my galleys back, and I need to get to work."

Addie kissed his cheek. "All right. I'll probably ask her to meet me for lunch to tell her in person. You sure you don't want to go?"

"Nah. You tell her. Just promise me you'll count how many times she says 'good gravy' during the conversation. That's so important!"

"She really needs to be a character in a book. Too bad you don't write romance!"

"I'm not starting either!"

Meddling in Manhattan

Made in the USA
Middletown, DE
17 April 2022